THE 'K' ASSIGNMENT

America in the early sixties, a nation slowly thawing out its Cold War opposition to Communist Russia. But there are some people who refuse to unfreeze. Like Walt Connell and his patriot force, the Sons of America. Connell is ambitious, he has big plans. And when the Russian leader 'K' attends a peace conference in New York, Connell puts them in motion. At his right hand is a man whom Connell trusts completely. That's his big mistake. When you're going to kill somebody as important as 'K' you shouldn't trust anyone at all . . .

THE 'K' ASSIGNMENT

Leslie Waller

ATLANTIC LARGE PRINT

Chivers Press
and
John Curley & Associates Inc.

Library of Congress Cataloging in Publication Data

Waller, Leslie, 1923–
  The 'K' assignment.

  (Atlantic large print)
  Reprint. Originally published: London:
  Mayflower Books, 1976.
  1. Large type books. I. Title.
[PS3545.A565K2 1982]   813'.54   82–1372
ISBN 0–89340–460–8   AACR2

British Library Cataloguing in Publication Data

Waller, L.
  The 'K' assignment.—Large print ed.—
  (Atlantic large print)
  I. Title
813'.54[F]   PS3545.A565

  ISBN 0–85119–507–5

This Large Print edition is published by Chivers Press, England, and John Curley & Associates, Inc, U.S.A. 1982

Published by arrangement with Granada Publishing Limited
Previously published under the title 'K'

U.K. Hardback ISBN 0 85119 507 5
U.S.A. Softback ISBN 0 89340 460 8

THE 'K' ASSIGNMENT

CHAPTER ONE

The shouting and wildly hysterical applause distracted Ryder and he failed to notice the man in the first row.

Although the auditorium was not one of Chicago's largest, on this occasion it was one of the city's most crowded. Walt Connell had estimated the audience at well over fifteen thousand overheated people, sweltering in August weather; a crowd big enough for New York's Madison Square Garden at the very least.

Facing them now, Connell crouched at the lectern, cheeks rank with sweat, heavy arms shoved high, voice howling and raised to a thunderous peak by the public address amplifiers. Ryder sat well back from him, to his left, far out of the intense pinpoint of light where the two spots crossed beams and picked out Connell's face like the rare specimen that it was. It was Ryder's job to avoid spotlights, just as it was Connell's to bask in their hot glare.

'. . . And I say to you that we will—yes, we will—we can, we must rise in the mighty anger of our wrath,' Connell was shouting, 'and waken a sleeping America to the insidious dangers that stalk our land. We, the United Sons of America, have sworn a mighty pledge to . . .'

The man in the first row moved forward a yard on a slight diagonal. His motion finally attracted Ryder's attention. Squinting against the blinding light, Ryder saw that the man was short and wiry and carried something in his hand. Ryder got slowly to his feet and eased his way sideways toward the far end of the podium.

'. . . Return our glorious Motherland to the mighty place from which she has been toppled—oh, so insidiously—by the faint of heart and the fuzzy of mind. Together, the Sons of America will march forward . . .'

Even as he slipped around the podium and down the stairs to the orchestra section, Ryder wondered how many times tonight Connell would use 'mighty' and 'insidious'—his two favorite words. As a public speaker, Connell was the best. He projected emotion the way a firehose squirts water. But the Sons would never appeal to anyone with a real mind, Ryder decided, as long as Connell refused to take the trouble to clothe some original thoughts

2

in some original language.

The man who had gotten up from the first row of seats now stood frozen in a peculiar pose, head sunk on his chest, eyes downcast. Ryder inched up slowly behind him.

'. . . Fake liberals, do-good pinkos, and the rest of the insidious crew who work like termites, gnawing from within the mighty bastions of . . .'

Ryder suppressed a smile. He would have to talk to Connell about his choice of words, not that it had done any good the last time he had spoken about it. 'Take the college boys, Johnny,' Connell had told him. 'I'll take the dumb-bunnies, the slobs, the mouth-breathers who never got beyond high school. I'll keep saying "mighty" and "insidious" till they stop believing anything else.'

'But you and I are intelligent and loyal Americans,' Connell was telling the mouth-breathers now as Ryder inched up behind the man. 'We know what can and must be done to wipe out this insidious plot. We know how to . . .'

Suddenly Ryder saw that the thing in the man's hand was a camera, a twin-lens reflex. He was staring down into the focussing hood. Ryder closed the gap between himself and the man. His movement attracted the photographer's attention. He whirled around, backed away. A flash bulb exploded in Ryder's face.

He jumped at the man, hands clutching. The man turned to run. Two of Connell's beefy guards lumbered toward Ryder from the far side of the hall. The photographer was trapped.

He spun sideways and launched a kick at Ryder's groin. Ryder jumped back. A hot, red ball was etched on the retina of his eye. He shifted sideways and rammed the toe of his shoe into the photographer's shin, dumping him to his knees. Ryder snatched up the camera, broke it open and let a flesh-coloured roll of film unreel into the light. The two bodyguards grabbed the photographer under his armpits, hoisted him into the air and held him struggling there.

'Even here!' Walt Connell howled, 'even in our very midst, the enemy sends agents, spies to harass our mighty forward march. But these insidious infiltration tricks cannot work. Take him away, boys, back to his Kremlin-loving friends. And now, to you loyal Americans, I say . . .'

Ryder directed the guards and their burden to a small backstage room. The photographer was gasping for breath as they slammed him down into a rickety folding chair.

'Who sent you?' Ryder barked.

The man coughed with the effort of breathing and rubbed his chest.

Ryder reached into his breast pocket and pulled out a wallet, flipped it open and found a press pass issued to a George Newton of the *Weekly Forum*.

'It takes real nerve,' Ryder said, laughing. 'The *Weekly Forum* is not exactly one of the favorite news magazines of the United Sons.'

'Womme t'take care've'm?' one guard asked.

Ryder shoved the wallet back in the photographer's coat pocket. 'Hold it,' he ordered, dipping his fingers into the man's pockets. 'Stand up.' He fanned the photographer's hips and legs. Tucked in one sock, Ryder found a tiny Minox camera. 'My congratulations, Mr. Newton,' he said, shucking the camera open and removing the film. 'You're awfully damned resourceful, aren't you?

5

Was the Rollei a decoy? Was I supposed to miss this little baby?' He handed it back empty. 'Get him out of here, boys.'

'C'n I work'm over?' one guard asked.

'Not tonight. This is a gentleman of the press, boys. At the moment we have freedom of the press in this country. He's free to go, minus his film.'

Newton stood up and straightened out his clothes. 'I don't get you people,' he complained. 'Why so camera-shy? You all got police records or something?'

Ryder smiled pleasantly. 'You have plenty of pictures of Mr. Connell,' he told the photographer. 'He's the only one of us who counts. Now, quit while you're still ahead. Get moving.' He shoved Newton gently toward a rear door.

Once Newton and the guards had left, Ryder stood quietly for a moment, evaluating the incident. With D-Day less than a week off, he could afford no last-minute errors. And yet, as he knew from experience, it was always at the very end, when the tension of waiting mounted unbearably, that the sillier mistakes were made.

Had this been Newton's mistake, or Ryder's? The open attempt to take a flash

6

picture of Connell—of whom thousands of photos already existed—had either been stupid or very clever. Obviously Newton had already exposed a series of Minox photos, but the negatives were so tiny that they rarely made blow-ups good enough for use in a magazine. Newton had probably thought it was worth a try getting a shot with the Rollei; the worst that would happen was that he would be chased out of the place with his Minox pictures intact. Unless . . .

Ryder had moved to the door leading back into the auditorium. He stopped and stood perfectly still for a moment as he considered a new thought: what if Newton had taken one roll of Minox pictures, hidden it and reloaded? The exposed spool was as small as a thimble. He could have hidden it successfully almost anywhere that a quick search would fail to reveal. In which case, Ryder decided, Newton had just been escorted to freedom carrying some damned embarrassing photographs. And D-Day was in four days.

In what seemed like the far distance, with the thundering like a great, rushing cataract of water, Ryder could hear the prolonged and mounting applause that meant Connell had finished his speech.

Moving quickly now, Ryder walked back onto the platform. The applause hit him as forcefully as if he had walked full tilt into a brick wall. He paused for a moment, then eased in behind Connell. It was like stepping into a hot bath with the man. The fever of the audience's wild approval washed over Ryder and Connell, ebbing and flowing, wave after wave.

As he had so many times in the past year, Ryder found himself wondering what caused his tumultuous outpouring, what secret spring Connell always managed to tap in his audiences, loosing this gusher of emotion.

'And now,' Connell began. He paused, waited. 'And now...' Again he waited as the applause slowly, reluctantly grew less fierce. 'And now, loyal friends...' This time the noise subsided to a level where Connell would quench it simply by talking over it.

'And now, my good and loyal friends, I would like to present one of my trusted associates, a true friend of liberty with an important message for all of you. Friends ... Johnny Henderson!'

The stingy spattering of applause pleased

Ryder as he replaced Connell at the lectern. He had no intention of drawing approval as deafening as that accorded Connell. Nor did he intend that Connell suspect the man he knew as 'John Henderson' of being anything but a 'good and loyal friend.'

As Ryder began his well-rehearsed appeal for funds, before the ushers passed collection boxes, he found himself remembering the photographer and the Minox and the question of whether there had been a hidden spool of film, he had neglected to find. The thing would have been dangerously easy to overlook in a moment of carelessness.

This late in the game, Ryder thought, so close to the end, with the job only a few days from completion, he could not afford to grow careless. It could mean his life, at the very least, and the lives of others as well.

There was simply no margin for error.

CHAPTER TWO

The house was old and well-constructed, built in the heyday of Chicago's Gold Coast when robber-baron fortunes in steel and beef and wheat had made the Near North Side one of the most ostentatious and expensive areas in the country.

Yet now, more than half a century later, the only thing that distinguished this large and rather elegant house from the somewhat Bohemian neighbourhood in which it stood was the fact that it had its very extensive and well-tended grounds.

A fifteen-foot-high wrought-iron fence with spiky finials surrounded close-cropped lawns which were strangely barren of trees or shrubs. As Ryder stared out a third-floor window toward Lake Michigan, he noted in the fading evening light how little cover the grounds provided for anyone hoping to enter the house by stealth. He supposed it was in the warped nature of Old Man Hungerford, whose family had owned the place for many generations, that he had cleared off any foliage precisely to discourage burglars or Communist spies or labor organizers or champions of fluoridated water or any of the other bogeymen who infested his troubled sleep.

Since Hungerford had placed the entire house and several of his millions at the disposal of the United Sons of America he could not have planned more brilliantly for the organization's security, Ryder decided now as he eyed the bare lawns surrounding the house.

'Johnny?'

Ryder turned from the window. He watched Walt Connell's fleshy face for a moment. 'Just checking the grounds, Walt.'

'Jumpy?'

'This close to D-Day yes. That photographer the other night.' Ryder sighed impatiently. 'Should have nailed him before he got that close but the lights blinded me. I didn't see him till he was practically on top of you.'

'Just a snooper, Johnny.'

'He might've been carrying a gun instead of a camera.'

Connell laughed. 'Who'd want to kill me? The Commies don't operate that way, no matter what I tell the slobs, Johnny. Don't start believing everything I say, huh?'

'He could have made trouble.'

'Could have,' Connell agreed. He grunted slightly as he lowered his bulky frame into a padded chair. 'Anyway, I got

11

bodyguards for work like that. You're my brain guy, Johnny, not my muscle man.'

'I can handle muscle, too.'

'Well I know it.' Connell sighed happily. 'Three more days to go, buddy. And then. *Der Tag.*'

Ryder winced at Connell's flat, Midwestern, mispronounced German. Anyone who borrowed so much strategic know-how from the Nazis could at least bother to learn how to speak the mother tongue. Ryder sat down across the table from Connell. 'This is Wednesday,' he said. 'Tomorrow I fly to New York and check into the Waldorf. And then . . . Friday!'

'God, you youngsters are impatient.' Connell chuckled softly.

Ryder frowned. At thirty-seven he had no illusions of being a youngster. It irked him to be patronized by Connell, who himself was no more than forty-four. 'All right, old man,' he responded. For a moment he saw that Connell took him seriously. Then the fat man's mouth parted in a pursy smile.

'I am the Old Man of this outfit, that's for sure. And you'll take your orders from the Old Man. Right, Johnny?'

'Absolutely!'

'Then my order is to forget Thursday, forget New York, forget the Waldorf and forget Friday, too. We've got a good plan and good equipment. It'll go off like a Swiss watch. You'll see.'

'How good are those grenades?'

'Like new.'

'Army surplus isn't my idea of perfect condition.'

Connell leaned back easily. 'Will you let the Old Man do the worrying? I didn't exactly have them bought at some corner Army-Navy store. They're brand new, right out of Quartermaster's, and the cordite's been replaced with GS-2.'

Ryder looked worried. 'Tricky. Does it detonate as reliably as cordite?'

'Didn't I tell you to let me do the worrying? It detonates like a dream and the explosive strength is triple cordite's. That ups the shrapnel burst from a twenty-foot circle to about forty-five feet.'

Ryder lighted a cigarette. 'What about Craigie's stuff? Serial numbers?'

Connell shook his big head slowly. 'One of our people out in Denver gave me a hell of an idea once. He'd done a stretch in stir and knew the whole technique. Got it from his cell mate. We took Craigie's rifle and hand gun and filed off the serial numbers. Then the boys in the shop hammered in some new dies with conflicting numbers. They filed the new ones off, too.' Connell began to chuckle again. 'We'll see what the New York cops or the FBI can make of that.' His portly frame began to shake with laughter.

'Ought to slow them up nicely,' Ryder said.

'Even with the CIA or the Secret Service boys,' Connell said, 'the only way they can reproduce filed numbers is by etching. Sure, they'll bring up the old numbers. But the fake ones will come up just as strong. It'll be a lovely mess. By the time they sort out the numbers and check 'em with the manufacturers, Friday will have come and gone. The rest, Johnny, will be history.'

'By the time they trace the guns to us,' Ryder mused, 'we won't care if they do.'

Ryder blew cigarette smoke at the carved oak ceiling overhead. 'The rest is for the history books,' he said then. 'You're right, Walt. This thing will go into every history book for centuries to come. It has to.'

'And yours truly, Walt Connell, along with it.'

'And the Sons.'

'And the Sons,' Connell repeated in a voice that had grown solemn. 'By God, what a plan, Johnny. What a blow!'

'I've been over the plan a hundred times,' Ryder said. 'I can't see any place we could slip up.'

'There isn't any,' Connell assured him. 'A chance like this comes only once to a man or an organization. If we muff it, we die. But, Johnny, if we make it...' Connell's eyes hooded. He got up and paced to the windows, staring out into the night at the almost invisible lake beyond the Outer Drive. 'I'll tell you my personal belief,' he said in a strong, low voice. 'If we make it, Johnny, this whole goddamned nation is *ours*.'

Ryder felt the skin across his shoulders creep sideways. He knew Connell for a clever man and a brilliant one. He also knew him for a man consumed by sick, arrogant ambition. Yet it was not entirely too much to believe, with Connell, that what they would do on Friday in New York could conceivably play right into the sick ambitions of others, of millions of others. Was Connell's belief a sick one? Was his certainty the product of his brilliant mind or his sick mind?

The intercom buzzer interrupted Ryder's thoughts. Connell turned from the window and flicked down a switch. 'Connell here.'

'Commander Connell.' The elderly maiden lady who handled the switchboard contributed twenty dollars a week to the United Sons for the privilege of putting in a ten-hour day at the board. 'A woman calling, Commander. Something fishy. Thought you should know.'

'What's she want?'

'Wants to speak to somebody named Ryder. John Ryder.'

Ryder's face frowned. But his heart constricted into what felt like a tiny ball of lead. He could feel the muscles in his back and legs tense for action. Slowly, methodically, he relaxed them. His cover was too good. A year's careful work could not be uncovered by a random phone call.

'Ryder?' Connell echoed. 'We have no Ryder here at HQ, do we?'

'I told her that. She insists we do.'

Connell glanced at Ryder. 'Ring any bell, Johnny?'

Slowly, Ryder shook his head. 'There's a Rydell in our South Side Chapter. And out

16

in Iowa we have a cell captain named, uh, Ridenbeck.'

'Ask her who she is,' Connell told the intercom.

'One moment, Commander.' The speaker went dead, then crackled into life again. 'Says her name is Culhane. Constance Culhane. From that pinko sheet, *Weekly Forum*.'

'Tell her to go . . .' Connell stopped himself. 'Hang up on her. She's one of these insidious agitators.'

'Right.' The intercom went dead.

'*Weekly Forum* again,' Connell muttered. 'First the photographer, now somebody with a phony story. Probably on a fishing expedition. Name Ryder mean anything to you?'

Ryder shrugged. 'If it isn't *Time* or *Newsweek* or one of the other rags,' he said, 'it's the *Weekly Forum*. We know what to expect from that kind of reporter. Let's just forget it.'

'It's forgotten.' Connell turned back to the dark window.

He propped his bulky body against the window frame and stared out into the night. 'It's out there, Johnny,' he said after a moment. 'You know the lake is out there, almost close enough to touch and feel, even if you can't see it. That's what Friday's like—almost within reach. A single day in our lives and the whole country to win. Maybe even the world.'

Ryder inhaled cigarette smoke and blew it out in an uneven, jerky stream, marred by the shaky action of his lungs.

The thing that had just—almost!—happened was impossible to dismiss as a coincidence. The photographer had—must have!—hidden a spool of Minox film on which he had surreptitiously taken pictures of the speaker's platform the other night. Back in New York the film had been cooked to compensate for underexposure, then enlarged.

Ryder closed his eyes, picturing the scene. Editorial conference. Reporters and writers around the table. Photographs passing from hand to hand. One woman looking casually at the pictures. Suddenly, she looks more closely. 'That one, there. The man sitting next to Connell, Even with that moustache, he looks familiar.'

Ryder opened his eyes. This close to the end he had been unforgivably careless. He could not let this mistake endanger a year's work.

Wherever Connie Culhane might be—probably right here in Chicago—she would have to be found and put out of the way . . . fast.

'Johnny,' Connell said lazily, 'mix us a drink.'

CHAPTER THREE

At three in the morning, Ryder walked slowly but steadily along the hot, dark street. As he neared the building that had been his home for nearly a year he fought off the faint nausea he always had when returning to this place.

Tall, pinched-looking, dingy, the building looked more like a private apartment house than the residential hotel it actually was. Yet its narrow, constrained look was not what Ryder objected to. Rather it was the feel of the place and its reasons for being: a refined, restricted mausoleum where old people with some wealth sat around to wait for death.

Placed there by dutiful children, the guests of the hotel kept up the careful fiction that they were much better off living this way than in a home for old people. But it was no place, Ryder reflected as he turned into the doorway, for anyone under sixty. It was especially no place for a single person with things on his mind.

Ryder passed the small, aging homosexual who served as night desk clerk. His cheeks faintly rosy with rouge, the little man snored genteelly, head propped on one hand.

The elevator door was open and the car empty. Somewhere in the building the operator whiled away the small hours of the night in drink and sleep, secure in the knowledge that none of the guests would need his services at this hour.

Ryder glanced at his watch. Three-ten. Connell had insisted on a great many drinks and a great deal of his grandiose talk. The man seemed afraid to be alone with himself this close to the moment of his triumphant self-sacrifice. Ryder had finally gotten away from him on the pretext—which happened to be true—that he had to be at O'Hare Airport early the next morning for the New York flight. But, meanwhile, precious hours had been wasted during which Ryder had been unable to do anything about the problem of Connie Culhane.

Deciding not to buzz for the missing elevator operator, Ryder mounted the narrow stairway that spiraled upward around the shaft. On the third floor, a bit winded, he walked down a badly lighted corridor. A year of this kind of work, he mused, with its sedentary ways, its late hours, its heavy drinking and eating, had put him so far out of physical condition that he was almost afraid to think of the regimen of workouts he would have to put himself on after Friday.

Assuming, he thought suddenly, he was still alive after Friday.

Although he knew that the ancient Oriental carpeting underfoot was vacuumed each morning, Ryder could still smell the strong, dusty odor that pervaded the hallway. As he stopped at his door, he recognized the odor. It was not the dust, nor was it the furniture polish, nor the insecticide.

It was the smell of death, waiting for the guests of the hotel as it waited, too, for him.

He unlocked his door, went into his room, and locked the door behind him, latching the special bolt as an added precaution. He sniffed. The room stank of

21

the same charnel smell. Ryder's nose wrinked. Was death, he wondered, as close to him as to the other guests in this stinking place?

Hurrying now, he strode through the darkened living room to the bathroom, turned on the shower, and stripped off his clothing. Under the icy water he felt his blood begin to race through his body, giving the lie to the stench of death.

Funny, he mused as he dried himself off. He rarely thought of death. In his line of work one didn't.

Still drying himself, he padded slowly into the living room toward the liquor cabinet. The drinks with Connell had only deepened Ryder's disgust. One or two more might push him over the edge into mindlessness and sleep. As he pulled the cork from a bottle of Scotch, the room blazed with light.

He whirled around. Connie Culhane stood in the doorway to his bedroom, her hand on the light switch.

'Good evening, John Ryder.'

Slowly Ryder put down the bottle. He picked the towel off the chair where he had thrown it and, still moving slowly, draped it around his midriff. His eyes remained on the woman in the doorway. She had lost quite a bit of weight. The last time he'd seen her, only a year after the war, she had been nineteen and her cheeks had been smoothly full. They were hollow now under wide, huge eyes that looked tired with things they'd watched. Her hair had been dark blonde in that faraway time. It was bright, ashen gold now, curled short with careful carelessness, an expensive hairdo and no longer a youthful one. He remembered her lips as being lush and full. They were slender now, racier. He frowned.

'You'll forgive me,' Ryder said in a cold voice. 'I usually dress to receive strange...'

'You wouldn't talk to me when I called you earlier this evening.'

Her voice was almost the same, he noted, but deeper now and somewhat hoarser as if, like her eyes, it had grown tired of many things. 'How did you get in here?' Ryder asked. 'Who are you?'

She shrugged. Her breasts, still as full as he remembered, moved in a slow, controlled arc. 'It was surprisingly easy. I told them the truth at the desk. I said I was an old friend of Mr. John Henderson.'

'And they believed you?'

'People usually know when you're telling the truth.'

'I've never seen you before in my life,' Ryder told her with flat, careful concentration. Tone was important, he reminded himself; too vehement a tone would make her suspicious. 'Now, then, whatever your game is, I'm not playing. The front door's there. You can leave under your own power.' He moved toward the house telephone. 'Or I can have you put out. Choose.'

'I've seen your desk clerk,' she said, smiling. 'You'd have to do better than that to frighten me.'

'Will the police do?'

'There you're overreaching, Johnny. Call the police, and I insist you're not John Henderson. My magazine insists you be checked. When they do, your masquerade goes poof, despite that silly moustache you've grown. So forget the phone. I'm here only to talk, Johnny, nothing more.'

'Do we have anything to talk about?' Ryder asked. 'We haven't met before.'

'Not in years,' she amended. '1946, Johnny. October 14, 1946. I believe it was shortly after eleven at night that we . . . uh

24

. . . parted?'

Ryder grinned. 'I see what it is now. You're a looney. Is that it? A looney with one of these complicated stories? Looneys work out all the little details. Hour, day, moustache. They're good at it.'

'You insist you're not John Ryder?'

Ryder walked back to the liquor cabinet. 'I am not, nor have I ever been, John Ryder. Now then, who are you? What are you doing here?'

She sat down suddenly in a straightbacked chair, as if her strength had abruptly left her. 'I work for *Weekly Forum*, Johnny. You've seen my by-line?'

'I've seen the *Forum*. Tangled with one of your photogs the other night. What's the plot? Is he supposed to burst in here and snap a picture of us in a compromising situation?' He glanced down at his towel. 'If so, shouldn't I get you a towel?'

She started to speak, then seemed unable to get the words out. Her eyes flicked sideways at his hands as he poured himself a straight Scotch. 'May I have one?'

He handed her the drink. 'Nerve gone?'

She sipped the whisky. 'Johnny, what's happened to you?'

'Sorry.' He poured himself a long shot.

25

'Drink your drink and beat it. There's no story tonight.'

'You were never this way before.'

'True. I never was. You never were. None of this existed before you and your idiotic magazine put this little sketch together.'

She shook her head with slow sadness. 'I mean it, Johnny. You were not this kind of man before. You were warm and loving and interested in life.'

'All that? Hell of a fella.'

'Now you're sealed-off, walled-in. You just ... just don't relate to me or people or the world, do you?'

'I relate to *my* world,' Ryder snapped angrily.

'What kind of world is that? A hate-filled world, full of ranting and threats? Walt Connell's world? Is that yours, too?'

Ryder's mouth quirked sideways, but he remained silent long enough to master and suppress the words she had almost jolted out of him. Instead he smiled lazily. 'Is there some other world, Lady Reporter? What's your world filled with? Bleeding hearts and milk for kiddies?'

'That kind of cheap sarc—'

'Intruders don't usually take that high

kind of tone,' Ryder cut in. 'You seem to have confused our roles. You broke in here. I live here. And now, without too much further ado, why don't you get the hell out?'

She stood up. Her glass, half-full, clinked hard as she set it down on the table. 'Yes, I think I will,' she said softly.

'You're allowed to finish your drink. In my hate-filled world, we still have manners. Do they in your world?'

'I don't drink with people I suddenly dislike.'

Ryder bowed slightly. 'Sound rule for a pretty woman. A very limited rule for a reporter. You must meet so many distasteful people in your world. Good-by, Miss . . . ?'

'It's Mrs.' Her eyes flashed upwards, paused as she watched him for an instant, then shifted nervously away. 'Mrs. Peters.'

Ryder felt the edges of his gut begin to gather slowly together. When people described this feeling they always remembered it as happening quickly. They were wrong. If it happened quickly, Ryder thought, you could get through and past and done with it. Instead, like a Venus's-flytrap closing on its prey, the

27

feeling seemed to enfold him with sickening slowness. 'Mrs. Peters?' he echoed, trying to keep his voice level and disinterested. 'I thought . . . ?'

'You thought I'd given the name of Culhane when I called before?'

Ryder swallowed. The tenderness in his stomach began to assume the agony of pain. 'Oh,' he said, trying to elude the trap, 'was that you?'

'I gave my maiden name so you'd remember. Peters wouldn't have meant much to John Ryder.' She smiled and started for the door. 'It was more than two years after that night in 1946, Johnny, oh, at least two-and-a-half years before I married Harry Peters. It took that long before I finally realized that you really, honestly, truly meant every horrible word you'd said about the two of us being totally washed-up. Can you imagine a bright girl like me being quite that stupid?'

Ryder tried to relax the muscle spasm across his midriff. It hadn't happened in years, but this damned woman had the power to make it happen again.

'Two-and-a-half years,' she was saying, 'of telling myself we'd been so perfect together—by day and by night—in bed and

28

out of it, that I knew you couldn't have meant all those things you told me. And then, after I hadn't seen you or heard from you, after all my letters came back, after you just seemed to drop off the face of the earth, I turned to Harry and . . .' Her voice choked out.

'Mrs. Peters.' The effort of forcing his voice to sound normal was almost too much for the knotted muscles in Ryder's viscera. 'Mrs. Peters, I don't see a wedding ring.'

'It was all right, for a while. Then it wasn't. After ten years we broke it up. No children so, of course, not much point in keeping it going.'

'Then you really aren't Mrs. Peters?'

She reached the outer door of the apartment. 'That should make little difference to a man who isn't John Ryder.'

He nodded. 'Good-by, then. Tell your boss it was grand, a story full of heart, moustaches, returned letters, a million laughs but just no dice. Tell him to stop sending his trained seals around. It's a waste of his money and my time.'

'You haven't heard the punchline.'

'Lay it on me, Lady Reporter.'

Her hand, on the doorknob, twitched slightly. 'As you wouldn't know, of course, this happened before the war. Connecticut. Small town on the Sound. Big high school hockey game. Our goalie had no use for padding. Reflexes like lightning. But this one night the other team used rough tactics. They ganged him at the goal. The sticks and blades were flashing. The coaches ran out to stop it. But this marvelous goalie of ours had gotten slashed, by a blade, I think. The doctor took fourteen stitches and it left a scar.' She touched his left shoulder. 'That one.'

Suddenly the knot in Ryder's stomach dissolved. He took her hand from the doorknob. 'Sit down and finish your drink,' he said.

'Did I pick the wrong way to remember you? Not romantic enough?' She sat down and watched him closely. 'Should I have remembered that small brown mole high up on your right thigh? Or the tiny tuft of hair at the small of your back?'

Ryder touched his shoulder. 'You never saw this scar before.'

'Quite true. It's been fiddled with, hasn't it? Plastic surgery . . . skin graft? But they couldn't distort the length or the curved shape of it. All they could do was cover over the stitch marks.' She paused.

'Darling,' she added with slight sarcasm.

'*Weekly Forum* hires bright people.' Ryder stood for a moment without moving. 'Too smart.'

'Smart enough to wonder why a man has a boyhood scar covered up. What kind of life makes it necessary to do that, Johnny?'

He grinned at her without speaking, mostly to disarm her and not because he felt mirth. What had to happen now, he reflected, was not very funny. Once Ryder realized that he could never convince her he was Henderson, Connie Culhane became a danger to herself.

'You wouldn't happen to have any of my boyhood dental X-rays with you?'

'That's not funny,' she said. 'None of this is. You're posing as someone; one of these hate merchants. But the real you, Johnny, doesn't seem to be that much different from the fake you.'

Ryder gestured negligently. 'Is anybody really who people think he is?'

She watched him for a long moment. 'Don't you know who you are any more?'

He shrugged. 'Now and then.'

She frowned. 'Are you trying to tell me . . . ?' She shook her head. 'You're not saying that you really don't know? Amnesia

31

sort of thing?'

'Nothing so handy. Look. I don't often entertain in just a towel. Will you excuse me while I put on some clothes?'

'I really don't intend to stay much longer. After I leave you can dress as you wish. As for the towel,' she paused, smiling slightly, 'I have any number of memories of you in which a towel would be considered overdressing.'

His eyes narrowed. 'Your imagination tends to veer toward the erotic. Have you had anyone look into it?'

Her face went blank. She stared emptily at him for a moment and then nodded slowly. 'Oh, yes. A woman who can't find satisfaction usually ends up in analysis.'

'And what did the good doctor tell you?'

She put down her drink and got to her feet. 'To find the man who did it to me.'

Neither of them spoke for a long moment. In the silence, Ryder could hear, far away and very faint, the lone hoot of an auto horn from the direction of the river. It had a mocking kind of sound.

'Who did it to you,' Ryder repeated then.

'Maybe not quite that,' she admitted. 'The man with whom I had something I never . . . quite found again.'

Ryder grimaced. He glanced at his wrist, but his watch was still in the bathroom. 'Time?'

She consulted her watch. 'Three-thirty. Why?'

'I have to think for a minute.'

'About what to do with me.' It was a statement, not a question.

'Yes.'

'Because I know who you really are.'

'Yes.'

'I don't really,' she said. 'Any more than you do, Johnny.' She sipped her whisky. 'Is it a matter of keeping my mouth shut? Because if that's what worries you, be assured I wouldn't dream of telling anyone that the love of my life had turned into someone like you.'

He made a disgusted face. 'Hold the rhetoric for a moment.'

'Is that what it sounds like to you?'

He sighed exasperatedly. 'Connie,' he began quickly with as much brutal offhandedness as he could manage to fake, 'we used to be great in bed, but don't mope through the years wailing that your sex life is ruined forever. Stop kidding yourself and your doctor and me and your ex-husband

33

and all the other lovers you've frozen up on. And for God's sake, stop talking. I have to think.'

He watched the effect of his words and felt a sharp pang of remorse when he saw her draw back as if slapped. Ryder found himself trying to remember the last time he had felt remorse. It had probably been on the night he had broken up their affair. And for what?

He turned to the mahogany writing desk and reached inside it for the outside phone he'd had installed on a direct line. Once a week, Ryder set his alarm for four in the morning. On such a day he would spend the next two hours with a flashlight, carefully tracing the line to this phone, tracking it floor by floor through the basement junction box to a sealed transformer tub in a house two doors down the block. From that point on, he knew, tapping his line would be a virtual impossibility. Once, six months ago, Ryder had found an induction tap on the back of the basement junction box. Instead of removing it, he had shifted it a half inch to one side, garbling his line with several others. A month later the tap was gone, removed by the man Connell had originally sent to install it, a bungler Ryder had since taken under his wing and taught the rudiments of his trade.

Since then no one had been interested in the line. Connell knew the private number, used it on occasion and seemed to take it for granted.

Watching Connie Culhane, Ryder now picked up the private phone and dialled a 703 code, followed by a number in Virginia. At this hour, no one at the other end would recognize his voice. But his signals had been recorded before, of course.

'Hello?' A man's sleepy voice.

'Ask Charlie to call his pigeon.'

'Hold it.' The line went dead for a moment. Then there was the faint crackle that told Ryder a recording device had been cut into the line and was feeding back a very faint signal. 'Hello? What the hell did you say?'

Ryder cleared his throat. 'Ask Charlie to call his pigeon. Then go back to sleep, you surly bastard.'

'What a grouch,' the man said.

'Soon,' Ryder snapped.

'Soon. Soon. Right.' The line went dead and Ryder hung up. Depending on where

Charlie was at the moment and whether he could be reached, the return call could take anywhere from minutes to hours. He glanced at Connie Culhane and found her watching him with rapt attention.

'Something wrong? Towel slipping?'

'What was all that?' she asked.

'Didn't you sort of notice? It was what we call, uh, making a phone call—on what we call the, uh, telephone.'

'But that was a long distance call.'

'God, you reporters are bright.'

'Is Charlie going to help you take care of me?'

'I hope so.'

She sipped her whisky. 'Why are you Charlie's pigeon? Is Charlie really Walt Connell? Has he left town? Is that it?'

'Umm . . . no.'

'Is Charlie someone higher up?' she persisted.

'Much higher up.'

She nodded. 'It always seemed obvious that Connell didn't have the brains to hold his organization together. For the last day or so I thought the brains might be you. But it's someone else, isn't it? It's Charlie.'

Ryder poured himself a new drink. He sat down across from the woman and crossed his legs, then hastily straightened out the towel. 'But while you're bright,' he said then with a nasty grin, 'you're never more than half bright. Why do you flatter yourself that only someone with a giant mind could create a United Sons of America? Why do you think, because you don't agree with a Walt Connell, because you hate what he stands for, that this automatically makes him a lamebrain?'

'Ah,' she retorted, 'I've been waiting for this. The justification. Let's hear you rationalize everything, Johnny.'

'I simply tell you,' he pointed out, 'that Connell has a first-class mind, whatever you think of his politics, and that even without such a mind, the Sons could have been successfully organized by just about anyone. They fill a need.'

'A place hate-filled people can spill out their hate?'

'Exactly,' he said. 'But climb down off your elevated niche long enough to understand hate-filled people. The whole world wants to know about people filled with love. Thousands of books and movies tell all about it. But no one bothers to find out about people filled with hate. And there are so many more of them.

'In this case,' he went on, 'it's lower middle-class people, caught in the pinch between the unionized working stiffs below them and the expense-account glamour boys above them. These little white collar people, shopkeepers, small-time self-employed people, none of them have the job security of the working stiff and don't even make his wages. But they're stuffed with stale dreams of some day becoming executives. They'll never make it. It's not in the cards.

'Once they feel this in their tired bones, the bitterness turns to bile. The hatred seeks scapegoats. Anything will do—the government, the Jews, the unions, the reds, the income tax, the UN, the Negroes, modern art, the Puerto Ricans, rock-and-roll music, the foreign-born—anything. Some of it's silly. But all of it's deadly.'

Her eyebrows went up. 'I'd no idea you knew your people so well as . . .'

The private phone rang.

Ryder sat without moving. After the first ring the phone was silent. Ryder began to count slowly in his head. When he reached sixty, the phone rang again. This time he picked it up. 'Yes?'

'Crazy?' a man asked.

'Coo-coo.'

'What's up, Pigeon?'

'See you in thirty minutes.'

'Kee-rist.' A pause. 'Make it forty?'

'Go man.' Ryder hung up.

He turned to look at Connie Culhane again. Her lips were slightly parted, as if to hear his conversation more clearly. 'The whole thing,' she said then in a wondering tone. 'Passwords, everything. You're Pigeon. So you say "coo-coo"—it's fantastic.'

Ryder got to his feet. 'We live in a fantastic world.' He took her arm and lifted her to her feet. Then his hand slipped down her wrist to the pressure point. He touched her skin there. She winced. 'This way,' he said, leading her into the bedroom. He snapped on the light and pushed her into a seated position on the bed. Then he pulled open a dresser drawer.

'Johnny, what . . . ?'

He showed her the gun, a snub-nosed .32 with a blued barrel and sight. Then he placed it on the dresser top, dropped his towel and pulled on a pair of shorts. He began to dress as rapidly as possible.

'That gun . . .' She seemed afraid to go on.

'Did you notice the mole?' he asked. 'Still there?'

'Johnny?'

'I can't really say I'm sorry about this,' he went on, buttoning his shirt and tucking it into his trousers. 'If you hadn't found me tonight I would have had to find you.'

Standing before the dull dresser mirror he shrugged into a shoulder holster, inserted the gun and adjusted the hang of the harness. After he put on his jacket he squinted at the drape of the cloth over the gun. 'Let's go.'

She stood up. 'What are . . .?'

He took her wrist and lightly pressed the come-along pressure point. Then he led her to the front door, unlocked it and swung it open. 'After you.'

Ryder hadn't taken this particular walk in several months. He made no point of keeping regular contact with Charlie who was, in any case, only for emergency use. But, because he had to know such things, Ryder knew that it took him no more than twenty minutes to walk from this dismal Near North Side hotel to the part of Michigan Boulevard that led past Tribune Tower.

The streets were empty of people at this

40

hour. Ryder paused at odd intervals to check his back trail, but found no one there. When they reached Tribune Tower, he forced her to wait for several minutes. An occasional car passed. Then Ryder led Connie Culhane down a flight of steps.

He could smell the water nearby. Picking his way carefully, he led them through the darkness under Michigan Boulevard, past parked cars and trash cans. Something rustled.

Ryder twisted sideways in time to see the long, slimy, gray trail of a rat disappear behind a crate stuffed with rotting orange rinds. The sweetish smell filled his nostrils. Nearby the river gurgled softly. Overhead a passing car sent a rumble through the blackness. In the distance, Ryder could hear the low-pitched throb of the *Tribune*'s presses.

He stepped over a cluster of rusting tin cans and stopped beside a deserted blue-and-white Post Office truck. For a long moment he scanned the darkness, watching for movement, listening for sounds. Then he checked his watch and led the woman behind the truck to a brick wall that had once been whitewashed. In the faint light, as his eyes adjusted to it, Ryder could read some of the obscenities scrawled on the flaking whitewash.

Faint now, but growing louder, Ryder could hear the soft purr of a car engine throttled down to just about idling speed. After a moment he heard the thin popping whisper of tire treads on cement. He pulled Connie Culhane close to him against his left side. The curve where her waist swelled into her hip seemed more abrupt than it had in those years long past. He could feel her muscles tense.

Fifteen feet away a large shape surged into view, stopped. A car door opened softly. Faint footsteps.

'Pigeon?'

'Back here, Charlie.'

A thin man materialized out of the darkness. 'Yes, Pigeon?'

'Present for you.' Ryder shoved the woman in front of him.

'Good grief!'

'Try that North Shore place.'

Charlie reached for Connie Culhane's hand. 'Come along, now.'

Ryder saw her twist sideways. 'No!' she yelped.

'Come on,' Charlie insisted.

'Help!' Her voice echoed deafeningly

under the low roof.

Ryder closed in behind her and fiercely mashed the palm of his hand into her mouth. 'Will you shut up?' he hissed.

'Tough one, huh, Pigeon?'

Ryder felt her lips part. An instant later her teeth closed on his skin. Pain shot up his arm. He pulled his free arm tight under her throat and began to apply growing pressure, cutting off her air. She gasped. Her body writhed, grinding her buttocks against his groin in an almost sexual movement. Then, relaxing suddenly, she dropped to her knees, breaking his hold.

'Help!' she screamed.

Ryder pulled his right hand back to his left shoulder, fingers locked. Swinging full, he chopped down hard behind her left ear.

Her body dropped to the cement. She lay there, motionless legs splayed out wide in a running position. For an obscure reason he had no time to analyze, Ryder knelt beside her and pulled her skirt down over her bare thighs. As he did so, her lips fluttered.

'Johnny . . . love.'

He stared at her face. Her eyelids twitched. Then she lay perfectly still. 'Sorry,' Ryder mumbled.

'Apologizing to me?' Charlie asked. 'I

like a nice pair of legs, too.'

'To her.' Ryder lifted her by the armpits, tucked his shoulder into her stomach and carried her to the waiting car.

'Friendly or foely?' Charlie asked as he got behind the wheel.

'Basically friendly.' Ryder busied himself by propping her up in a seated position beside Charlie.

'Gee, Pigeon, with a friend like you, a chick doesn't need any enemies.' Charlie laughed softly. 'Someone you know? Or just got in the way?'

'Both.' Ryder's mouth tasted dry and acrid.

'Old Flamesville?'

'Shut up and drive away, Charlie.'

'Coo-coo,' Charlie said mockingly. 'Okay, Pigeon, I guess you're entitled to nerves this close to *Der Tag*.'

Automatically, Ryder registered Charlie's perfect German pronunciation. 'I'm flying to New York later this morning. It's that close.'

'Give my regards to Broadway.'

'Go on, beat it.'

'I'll have to tell the Colonel about this chick.'

'Of course. Get going.'

Ryder watched him shift Connie Culhane into a more stable position beside him, her head against his shoulder. Then, headlights still dark, the car reversed direction and softly eased back along the passage down which it had come.

Ryder stood there in the darkness until everything was utterly silent. The taste in his mouth had grown metallic and ugly.

He began walking back to the hotel and its smell of death. Only the sound of his own footsteps and the faint scurrying of busy garbage rats broke the perfect silence of the night.

CHAPTER FOUR

After he had tipped the porter, Ryder saw that his was among the smaller of the Waldorf suites: a living room, a bedroom, and bath. He lay down on the couch and closed his eyes for a moment. Then he sat up slowly and reached for the phone. The air conditioning turned the August heat into a rather sterile May.

'Can I help you?' the operator asked.

'Outside line, please.'

He waited for the dial tone and, when he heard it, dialled a number slowly, pausing carefully between each digit. After a moment he heard the sound of the phone ringing. He let it ring three times in all, then hung up and lay back on the couch again.

For the first time in a year he let his mind wander.

It was usually a dangerous thing to do, he realized as he lay there now, but almost a year of intensive work seemed to him sufficient reason for indulging himself just this once. The next few hours were the last he would have completely to himself for some time to come.

It had been an unusual year, of that there could be no doubt. He had been resting at Montego Bay, sunning himself, swimming when the spirit moved him, and carrying on a rather pleasant affair with a single American woman who had the cottage next to his, when someone from Colonel Schroeder's office had checked into the main hotel and made contact at breakfast.

With the Colonel's man, he had flown back to home base in the States—that would be November of last year, he recalled now—and received a preliminary briefing. The Colonel explained that talk of a summit conference was more than just talk. His information was fairly clear on that point, if on little else. There would eventually be such a conference, the Colonel said, and the possibilities seemed to point, oddly enough, at New York as the place for it, in order to give the UN a certain amount of lip service. He felt it might take more than a year to come to fruition—and that was the end of the information.

Lying on the Waldorf's couch now, Ryder could recall that preliminary briefing with the trained, professional clarity that had, very probably, made them choose him for this particular assignment. He could remember the Colonel sitting there in an easy chair, a small man, partly bald, who had long ago affected a briar pipe for field work—because it went well with partial baldness—only to find, as the years went by, that he really liked pipe smoking.

'You understand, of course,' the Colonel had said in his quiet but perfectly audible voice, 'the tremendous risks of such a meeting in such a place, the crucial problems of security, lines of communication and command, the immense difficulty of developing any real strategy and the unfortunate necessity of improvising tactics almost on the spot. A very grave situation, and one our people will go to some lengths during the next year to avoid. Any European location will be bad enough. But New York itself . . . !' He had raised his hands from the arms of his chair and let them fall somewhat hopelessly back again.

'Do I understand,' Ryder began rather diffidently, 'that if New York is chosen you intend to pivot the operation around me?'

'In a manner of speaking.' The Colonel rapped his pipe into an ashtray and stared gloomily into the empty bowl. 'I take it you understand the primary fact.' He tamped tobacco in the pipe.

'Will K actually attend?'

The Colonel's match flared noisily, throwing his face into an odd, up-from-under light that made him look vaguely sinister. 'Yes,' he said, puffing on the pipe for a moment as he applied the flame. He sighed almost contentedly and smiled at Ryder again. 'I knew you would fit this operation like a glove. Your mind has just the proper kink to it.'

Ryder returned the smile. 'I take it the

kink matches yours,' he said.

'Then you're ready for assignment?'

'I think so.'

'No unfinished relaxation to take care of back in Montego Bay?' the Colonel added. 'Miss Giles, for example?'

Ryder sat back and lighted a cigarette. 'Unworthy of you,' he said then. 'Was my bedroom bugged? And if so, why?'

'Nothing so subtle. Five dollars to a bellhop.'

Ryder felt his ears and the back of his neck begin to grow warm. 'That's simply how it happened. You haven't yet said why.'

The older man said nothing for a moment. Examining his pipe, he saw that it had gone out. 'Now, look,' he said at last, 'you're about to become angry.'

'Perhaps.'

'That is a human luxury,' the Colonel said, striking another match.

'And?'

'And one,' the Colonel went on, punctuating his words with puffs of smoke, 'that you . . . cannot . . . afford.' He looked up at Ryder and opened his eyes very wide. 'Am I wrong?'

'Not wrong, if we're talking about

49

anger.' Ryder took a deep breath and felt himself steady down a bit. 'But what we were talking about was my privacy. I was off duty, you will remember.'

'Good,' the older man said in a polite, companionable way. 'Let's talk about duty, then. And whether one is ever really "off" it, as you say.'

Ryder sat back and said nothing for a long moment.

Resting on the couch in the Waldorf, he could remember quite precisely what had passed through his mind that moment almost a year before. It wasn't good, he told himself now, to be so bloody professional about one's own thoughts. There was no need to file them away so neatly for such ready reference. It was bound, as a habit, to be a bad one.

But yet, recalling how he had felt that day, he could see that there was really no answer to the Colonel's tidy little logical trap. For, of course, one was never really 'off' in this line of duty. And, given that as a premise, one's superiors had a professional duty to inform themselves of what one did in leisure time as well as on the job.

Duty, Ryder told himself now as he

stared up at the living room ceiling. It seemed to him like one of those words which, if you had time to spare, could be reduced to meaninglessness just by repetition. Duty. Doo-ty. Due-ty. He closed his eyes and, almost at once, the flood of thoughts he had been able to do without for the past year, washed up and over him in his self-imposed blindness.

Q—Duty to what?

A—To the job.

Q—Why?

A—Because it is important.

Q—To whom?

A—All right. To the country.

Q—Why?

A—Because one has to be born and live somewhere and there's no sense in asking why. And, that being so, one likes one's country to be strong and secure and prosperous.

Q—This 'one' you refer to—would you expand on that thought a little?

A—One? One is me.

Q—You are contributing to the strength, security, and prosperity of your country?

A—I . . . well, yes.

Q—Oh, good God, man, come off it.

Ryder opened his eyes wide, got up from the couch, and wandered into the

51

bathroom. He let the cold water run for a moment and stood there watching himself in the medicine-chest mirror. The skin of his upper lip, he noticed, was a bit lighter than the rest of his face, a heritage of the missing moustache. Silly damned thing. And he was picking up facial weight again. Too much all-night-diner eating. Silly damned business, he told himself, and a great waste of valuable time.

He filled a glass with water and drank it slowly, wondering what was so valuable about his time.

A—Nothing, really.

Q—Then will the witness kindly refrain from giving himself airs?

A—Yes, sir.

Q—Now then, this duty to which you refer, can you be a bit more explicit?

A—All of us have duties. I should think that was fairly self-evident.

Q—By 'all of us' you are alluding, I take it, to the average person?

A—To every person, average or exceptional.

Q—And in which category would the witness place himself?

Ryder filled the glass again and went back to the living room. He pulled the curtain aside and looked down almost sixteen stories onto Park Avenue. The evening sun was still fairly high in the west, but the Avenue was in shadow, cabs scuttling along it, jamming up, freeing themselves, dashing forward again.

The room was far too high, Ryder decided. Something on the fifth or sixth floor would have been less risky. Although August had been hot with little wind, even a small breeze could blow the grenade yards off target as it dropped from a window this high.

CHAPTER FIVE

Across the avenue, downtown a block or two, a great, busy hole in the ground replaced a building Ryder had once known.

He could no longer quite remember its name or even what it had looked like. But he knew that in other years he had been in and out of it several times, leaving behind a spoor that some super-bloodhound might have traced. No longer.

What traces of himself he had not personally erased, Ryder decided as he watched the gap across the avenue, had been ruthlessly abraded by his work. Now the Manhattan syndrome of construction-demolition-construction was wiping out even the physical things that belonged to his past.

Soon, Ryder reflected morosely, he would almost totally cease to exist in the way most people existed, leaving trails behind themselves.

In his own wake he left nothing any more. Like the tinsel chaff released by bombing planes to confuse enemy radar, Ryder usually left a trail of a carefully selected group of fictions. Like chaff, or the foam in the wake of a boat, it quickly disappeared from view, vagrant and short-lived.

Damn her.

With a great deal of caution and an emotion very close to fear, Ryder let his mind move backward for a moment and thought about Connie Culhane. She had had no right to re-enter his life at any time. But most especially she had chosen the worst possible time in doing it yesterday.

At once the vague fear in Ryder's mind and the anger it produced seemed to recede. He found himself making excuses

54

for her. She had had no idea, of course, what work he did. The long years of deliberate silence would have told her only that Ryder had no wish to make any kind of contact with her, but they could not in themselves have given her a clue to his reasons.

Yet, whether or not she understood the years of silence, Ryder decided now, she had no right to keep him somewhere at the center of her life after so much time had passed. It was abnormal. She, too, had created damnable fictions, fiercely forlorn, of the early, the first, the only love, the one that she could claim had spoiled her for another man. Nonsense, of course. Any normal, adaptable human being could forget it with time and move on to new relationships.

Ryder turned from the window and looked, without seeing, at the sterile bedroom. Aside from its bad effect on her, he thought, the dangerous thing now was how she had affected him.

They had had, it was true, a very complete affair, lasting from their late teens well into their early twenties when Ryder had returned to civilian life, seemingly no longer in the Army but, of course, not really a civilian either.

Over those years he and Connie had explored all the areas of love for the first time, feeling all the wonderfully painful side-effects of expectation, jealousy, longing, satisfaction. They had experimented together, pushing out to the perimeter of normal sexual experience. Ryder had done things with her he had never done with a woman since.

He winced and sat down slowly on the hotel bed, feeling the sudden quickening in his groin as a sign of weak self-indulgence. He sipped the cool water from his glass and marveled at how accurate a picture of advancing middle age he seemed to be presenting.

One thing was clear: he had to stop remembering. The memory of her was distracting in itself, Ryder realized, but distraction was only one of its dangers. A much sharper one was that he would want to admit her back into his life, in spite of the fact that he understood he could admit no woman for longer than a casual off-duty weekend.

Ryder closed his eyes and massaged his face with the palms of his hands. He had to put her out of his mind. If not, she represented an even more dangerous situation.

Other people, nine-to-five people with friends and lovers and acquaintances and colleagues, people with lives that developed in relation to the lives of others—such people had histories that moved forward in a give-and-take way. They affected the lives of others. Others affected their own lives. This was how normal people lived.

But his own life, Ryder decided now, had been thrust into deep-freeze such a long time ago. Since then he had led fictitious lives. The essential Ryder hibernated like an animal in the dim recesses of memory. The old Ryder, in fact, had almost become a kind of chilly dust. In a few years, Ryder saw, his own memory of himself as he had been, his vision of the real Ryder, would vanish completely.

How dangerous, then, that somewhere in this world was a full-blooded, living, breathing, fornicating Ryder preserved in the memory of a woman. Connie was the custodian of what he had once been. Her image of the old Ryder was still intact, as alive as if it presently walked the earth. This was the gravest danger she posed.

Ryder opened his eyes and stood up. He

paced to the window and stared south toward the demolished building. He realized that he had never before faced so formidable a situation. The enemy was as cunning as he because the enemy was himself.

He could feel his hand tighten around the water glass.

On pain of disaster and death he knew he had to pretend that Connie Culhane did not exist. It had been easy enough all these years. If he could bury her again, he could bury his old self in the same grave.

A wave of revulsion swept over him and he felt, for a moment, the same curdling spasm of his viscera. He lifted the glass of water. He could see that the surface of the liquid was trembling with the tension in his body.

For a moment he wanted to hurl the glass against the far wall. His mind shook so violently with the effort of control that water splashed on the floor at his feet. Grimly, he tried to relax. After a long, unhappy moment, he succeeded.

He felt fairly sure now that he could face tomorrow—*Der Tag*—with the cold mind necessary for success. There could be no failure. There was absolutely no alternative to success.

And yet, for a moment more, it was not easy to feel the grave close over him as it had many years before. But, because he had been trained well and demonstrated real aptitude for his work, Ryder was soon able to move past the quick moment of self-pity.

Self-pity, he thought giving a final moment to the problem, is for nine-to-five people.

He walked into the bathroom, returned the water glass to its shelf under the mirror, stared incuriously at his face for a moment and then returned to the living room to go over again in his mind the events of tomorrow, Friday, *Der Tag*.

CHAPTER SIX

At eight-thirty the suite of rooms was nearly dark. Ryder sat on the edge of the couch staring into nothing. He glanced at his watch and, seeing how late it was, reminded himself that he had neglected to flesh out his cover personality with anything like professional ability.

He picked up the phone and, when the operator answered, yawned rather loudly into it. 'Room Service, please,' he asked in a noticeably Midwestern voice, the r's hard as steel, the vowels short and tight. He remembered especially to shorten the double-o in 'room.' Silly, stupid waste of time, but once a professional, always a . . .

'Hello, Room Service?' He produced another gigantic yawn. 'This is Mr. Rutherford. Have you got a nice thick steak? Medium-well with baked potato and French fried onions? No salad, lots of coffee, and some lime jello with whipped cream. 'Got it? Okey-doke.'

He hung up and wondered whether he'd done it properly. The real menu, of course, would be breaded pork chops, French fried potatoes, lots of rolls and butter, and some kind of cream gravy, catsup on the side, and chocolate cream pie. But, after all, he was a man of some means: the taste for steak was definitely indicated. And what about that okey-doke?

Deciding that he was straining at gnats. Ryder turned on a light and quickly went to work on an imitation of a man just awakened from a nap. He opened the suitcase in one of the bedrooms and distributed some of the contents in drawers and closets, rumpled the bed, stripped off his jacket and tie and messed up his hair. Then, after removing his cufflinks, he took off his shoes and laid them at the side of the rumpled bed. He waited there, thinking about very little, until the waiter rang his bell.

Then, blinking and yawning, he stumbled to the front door and let the man into the darkened living room. 'Been catching forty winks,' he mumbled, reaching for the light switch.

'Will you dine in here, Mr. Rutherford?'

'Sure.' Ryder re-played the man's question in his mind for a moment, trying to place the slight accent.

'Smells great,' he said, hoping for another sample of speech.

'I hope you'll like it, sir.'

''Course we don't ship all the best cuts to New York, you know,' Ryder went on. 'We keep some of the good ones in Chicago, too.' He laughed in a meaningless way. What was the accent? Hungarian? Polish?

'Our chef prepares a delicious steak, sir.'

'Good for him!' Lithuanian? 'I hope it's medium-well.'

'Oh, certainly sir. When you ask for medium-well, sir, you are certain you will get it as you wish it, sir.'

Ukrainian? 'Say, how late does Room Service keep open?'

'All night, Mr. Rutherford.'

'No joke? You sleep here, huh?'

'Not me, sir. I go home.'

'Awful late work, even so. Got a long way to go?'

'To the Bronx, sir.'

Ryder laughed. 'Where's that?' Then, before the waiter could answer: 'Well, wherever it is, I wish you luck, boy. Who do I ask for when I want you again?'

'Peter, sir.'

'Okay, Peter, and if I want a few drinks later, you won't peter out on me, huh?' Ryder laughed uproariously, anxious now to get rid of the waiter. 'And, say, look, Peter, you know, I mean, the thing is I'm always ready for a little fun and frolic and if you have anything you want to suggest in the way of female . . .'

'I'm sorry, sir, but . . .'

'Right. Right-right-right. Absolutely. Okay, Pete.' He handed the man two dimes and closed the door after him.

Two dimes? It was in character with the

cover personality, Ryder decided, but it wouldn't exactly guarantee prompt service next time. He sat down at the table and lifted the covers off the food. The potato and onions he pushed to one side, reminding himself to get rid of them later down the toilet. His eating habits had grown so impossible in the last year that whenever he had the chance to eat alone he cut out starches completely.

Q—Did the sagging cheeks give you a scare?

A—At thirty-seven even a little sag is scary.

Q—All in the line of duty, eh?

A—Are we back to that?

Q—Have we ever left it? I regret, sir, that I have but one sag to give for my country. An exit line worthy of a modern hero.

A—I am no hero.

Q—You admit it?

A—I am a man doing his job.

Q—Then to what is your duty?

A—To the job.

Q—Ah, now that's a horse of another color.

He cut off a thin slice of his steak and tasted it. Although he hadn't had the opportunity to taste really properly broiled steak in nearly a year, he found now that he had very little appetite. He looked at his watch. Five to nine.

It was the result, he decided, of too much self-questioning. He had been warned about this from the very beginning, back in 1944, when Colonel Schroeder had first approached him in North Carolina. Ryder had been working in Special Services at an Air Force Technical Training Command field near Goldsboro. Schroeder had been a colonel then, as now, but in those days he had had a special unattached status involved with top echelon briefing of the units that were assembled at the field for shipment intact to other theatres of operation. Combat wings were put together in Goldsboro, complete with air crews, intelligence units, medical staffs, and even KP details, trained and sent overseas. And always, during the last week or two, the commanding officer of the outgoing unit, and his staff, would have some intensive interviews with Schroeder.

Trying to eat his steak, Ryder could remember fairly well his own initial interview with the Colonel and the order, even then, to question everything, anything, anybody, but never to question one's own motives.

He pushed the steak away from him and

sat there watching it. If he didn't eat most of it, Ryder realized, he would find it difficult to get rid of. He began slicing it deftly into long, thin strips. Then he cut the strips into segments of an inch in length. He was working very quickly with jagged, almost compulsive movements. Scooping out the baked potato, he broke it into small lumps and slashed the French fried onions into bits. Carrying his plate into the bathroom, he started shoving the food into the toilet bowl.

He would be hungry later, suspiciously hungry, but right now he had no appetite at all. Leaving some likely lumps of potato and pieces of steak fat on the plate, he flushed the toilet and returned to the living room.

God Almighty, he thought, sitting down at the table again and pouring a cup of coffee, this is a fine state of affairs. He glanced at his watch. Seven-past-nine.

He sipped the coffee black, found it too hot, and got to his feet. He was beginning to perspire slightly. Something was wrong.

Walking to the window, he stared down at the avenue and the lights of cars moving more swiftly along it now. He needed to evaluate his situation, seeking the thing that was wrong, that had taken away his appetite, that was causing him now to fall prey to several other minor kinds of anxiety symptoms: the urge to pace, a tendency to perspire, the desire to keep looking at his watch, the need to bring to a conclusion what lay ahead.

It was not, he told himself, as he worked back over his situation, the job he had done in Chicago or the business with Connie Culhane. It had been a good, solid job, a professional piece of work. His Chicago people were with him. Nor was it, he went on, the fact that tomorrow would bring to fruition a year's work on one of the most important operations the Colonel had ever designed. Ryder had worked as hard and as long on other operations. It was true, he added silently, that none of them had been quite like this one. But the magnitude of the planning could not, of itself, create the kind of thing that was now happening to him.

Q—May I suggest that the witness is misinformed?

A—You may.

Q—May I remind the witness that his past work has been, essentially, self-contained? That it began with him and, if it ended badly, was bad only for him?

A—True enough.

Q—But that the present work extends far beyond the witness? That it cannot end badly because it would be bad for many people in addition to the witness?

Ryder's eyes glazed as he watched the avenue below him. Yes, he agreed, the Colonel's planning had a kind of damned-if-you-don't quality about it.

'We have absolutely no margin for error,' he had said last November during the course of the second briefing. Ryder had spent the week between briefings doing intensive Chicago and mid-west research. He could locate himself on almost any street corner in Chicago and find his way to almost any other one; he knew all the hotels and theatres, most of the Loop bars and restaurants, all of the Hyde Park and Woodlawn neighborhood in and around the University where he was to live, plus the names and locations of all the suburbs and nearby towns.

'And when I say no margin,' Colonel Schroeder had said, 'I am fully aware of what it entails.'

'I'm afraid I don't,' Ryder had replied.

'You will, once we've unwrapped the

plan.'

Ryder had long ago cured himself of the need to know, as soon as possible, what the strategy might be. He sat back and grinned at Schroeder. 'When you say no margin for error,' he said, 'I assume you've thought of their people. They'll assign their best, of course.'

'No one who knows you, I don't think.'

'That's a safe assumption. I wasn't worrying about that. I was thinking of the general excellence of their work, especially in New York.'

The Colonel nodded and thought for a moment. 'You see, there is really only one way to guarantee success. We can't work this externally because it's too tightly shielded. It has to be done from the inside.' He looked up at Ryder. 'That's you. You move inside and work up fast.'

'Not much of a guarantee, though.'

'There are no guarantees in the sense of money-back-if-not-satisfied.' Schroeder agreed. 'The only guarantee is the ultimate one.'

Standing now at the window, watching Park Avenue at night, Ryder wondered if this were the factor that was creating anxiety. And yet how could it be? Every one of his jobs carried the same guarantee. The only reason his line of work could ever guarantee success was the ultimate reason.

That if and when it was needed to guarantee success, he or any of the rest, would sacrifice their lives.

Q—For what?

CHAPTER SEVEN

Ryder emptied the contents of his overnight cases, hung up the olive green suit in a closet and carefully distributed the shirts, underwear, socks and ties in two drawers of one of the bureaus in the bedroom he was using. After memorizing the contents of each and the order in which they had been arranged, he pulled both drawers out of the bureau and attached to their backs a tiny bit of what looked like brown masking tape. He kept his supply of what Colonel Schroeder referred to as 'tattletales' in a crumpled pack of cigarettes.

Sliding the drawers back into the bureau, Ryder picked up the phone, asked for Room Service and requested that the dinner things be cleared away.

He got ready to leave. The tattletales, together with the memorization of each drawer's layout, were not so much a way of knowing whether his room would be searched—since either method would give him the answer—but rather a kind of delicate gauge of the searcher's expertness.

It was not terribly important whether or not his room were searched, since nothing of interest was hidden in it and he carried his only weapon, Seconal, in his wallet. But someone in his line of work had to know the general identity of the searcher, the identity that could usually be deduced from the manner in which the search was carried out.

Hearing a discreet knock at the door, he let the waiter in. 'Hiya, Pete!' Ryder pounced. 'I thought sure they'd send a busboy or something. I guess I really rate around here, huh?'

'But, Mr. Rutherford, all our guests really rate.'

Polish or Ukranian? 'Going out on the town, Pete,' Ryder boomed. 'Yessir, gonna find myself a little excitement.'

He punched the waiter's arm very lightly just below the shoulder and noted with concealed surprise that the flesh was as hard as wood. Hand on the doorknob, Ryder took a quick inventory of the man: medium height, five-nine or ten; thick hair, cut short and greying at the temples; high forehead, deep-set eyes, slightly bulbous nose, wide mouth, large but not protruding chin.

'Take it easy, boy!' He slammed the door shut behind him and went downstairs to the lobby. The clock on the wall behind the reservation desk showed the time to be five minutes to ten. Ryder sat down in one of the chairs and waited.

At ten minutes after ten a short man arrived at the desk in the wake of a porter bearing four cases. His check-in accomplished, he drew a cigar from an inside pocket and started to unwrap it as he followed the porter past the sofa on which Ryder sat. The band from the cigar fluttered to the rug at Ryder's feet. Ryder ignored it, furious at the man's amateur idea of melodrama.

The man disappeared in an elevator and Ryder sat there for several moments more, wondering what insanity had prompted Craigie to drop the cigar-band. Ryder had worked with him almost constantly during

71

the past year, seeing him an average of three times a week. By tomorrow noon, Craigie would be in jail. If he had done his job well he would eventually draw a three-year sentence which, less good-behaviour time, would keep him out of circulation for nearly two years. But no one had forced him to volunteer for the job.

Trying to work up a decent counterfeit of emotion, in case he needed to play such a hand at a later time, Ryder got to his feet and wandered toward the Lexington Avenue side of the building, past Peacock Alley and out into the street. He strolled for a block or two, checking his back trail, until he came to the cigar store-luncheonette at Fifty-third Street.

Entering one of the phone booths, he dialled a number and let it ring. On the ninth buzz a woman's voice answered. 'H-hello?' Sleepy and a bit confused.

'Hi, honey, it's Pete.'

'Pete?' A yawn. 'Pete who?'

'Honey, it's Pete from the Bronx.'

'Petey! How are you?'

'I figured we could tie one on.'

'Where?' she asked, 'one of those creep joints of yours?'

'Strictly class, honey. Wherever you say.

Starlight Roof?'

'Sorry, Pete, I'm a busy girl. Give me a call some time.'

'Listen, honey, why don't we . . .?' The phone went dead in his ear. 'All right!' he barked. 'Big shot!' He hung up the phone and left the store. Turning up Fifty-third Street, he walked toward Park Avenue again, killing time. It generally took Honey and Company a good fifteen minutes to run any decent kind of check. He wandered past the Seagram Building's vertical bronze façade, all the floors ablaze in its forty stories, a tall oblong of light in the pleasant August evening. The plaza's fountains were turned high, their multiple jets sending a curtain of white water hissing upward into the night to fall back in whispers against the shallow flatness of the pool.

Ryder sat down and watched the fountains. What did it take, he asked himself, to be a Frank Craigie? The background of the man he knew, had known even before he'd come to Chicago for the purpose of meeting him. Craigie's story was commonplace, boring: forty-three, a divorced man with no children, manager of a chain shoe store on Fifty-fifth Street in the Hyde Park section, high-school graduate; nothing but commonplaces.

And yet at ten tomorrow morning, some five hours before the arrival of the Russian delegation at the Waldorf, Craigie would 'ineptly' reveal himself as a man planning to assassinate K. In the room the hotel police would find a 30–30 deer rifle with telescopic sights, a snub-nosed .32 revolver, both with filed numbers, and a tablet that lab analysis would reveal to be strychnine sulphate.

By eleven Craigie would be booked and held, the newspapermen would have been threatened with everything in the books to maintain silence and yet it would have leaked—because they made it their business to attract such leaks—to Soviet headquarters on the floor below the suite in which Ryder was staying.

Craigie's apparently abortive effort would relieve Sovint's collective mind, allay the darkest fears of the city police and make the Secret Service boys feel a little happier about the day's assignment. There would be no assassination attempt on K. In his suite on the floor below Ryder, K himself would probably breathe somewhat easier, although he was probably too old a hand at this sort of thing to think he was in the clear. And yet he had to rely on his Sovint boys as fully as Kennedy did on his own guardians.

It was an act of faith, Ryder thought as he watched the play of the fountains, that heads of state must perform. You had to have that enforced faith in your own intelligence people so that you could project the confident posture of triumph from the rear seat of an open Cadillac or Zis; the crowds cheered, arms waving, and one of them surely clutched a grenade, but you were forced to swallow thoughts like that because the posture was everything, everything.

Ah, civilization! Ryder closed his eyes for a moment and listened to the chuckling whisper of the water.

Stupid, hate-knotted Craigie, he mused. Not really a human being at all. More, he decided now, like the carefully preserved hull of a human being, neatly lacquered with commonplaces and filled to the brim with paranoid hate.

It must be a special kind of hatred, Ryder thought, that can send a man to jail so willingly, in order that another can be clear to do the job; that kind of fanatic compulsion makes martyrs for every cause, Commie or anti-Commie. A special kind of insanity, it feeds on plots—and plays with idiotic cigar-bands.

Listening to the fountain, Ryder felt his spirits drop alarmingly, not at the thought of Craigie, but at something else, something he could not place for a long moment. He opened his eyes and stared upward at the towering thrust of the bronze building, jutting into the night sky, its sides slashed forty times by hot streaks of light.

What is it now, he asked himself, what's the trouble?

He had to stop this kind of introspection. Especially now, it was the worst sort of danger to risk. He had to turn it off. But before he did, as the last act of a thinking animal, he had to know what it was about Craigie that disturbed him so.

It came to him slowly from somewhere so far inside him, so unused a faculty, that he could almost sense the feeling itself forcing upward through carefully nurtured layers of insulation.

He was jealous of Craigie.

Twisted with hate, eager to sacrifice himself so that Ryder could carry on in the clear, a stupid, self-destructive excuse for a human being, Craigie was still filled with something, something poisonous, but something.

And I, Ryder told himself now, am empty.

He got to his feet and glanced at his watch. Enough time had elapsed. He started back toward Lexington, moving more quickly now. Craigie's face, remembered from hundreds of evenings together in bars, at other people's homes, in offices, seemed to hover over the sidewalk. It grew larger, then dwindled, then swelled again and seemed about to burst apart.

Ryder stopped and blinked his eyes shut as hard as he could, then resumed walking. The face was gone.

He found a drugstore on the way back to the Waldorf and dialled a new number in the phone booth. It was answered at once by a man. 'Yes?'

'Pete from the Bronx,' Ryder said quickly.

'Employed sixteen months ago, single naturalized citizen,' the voice rattled on at a fast clip, 'no record but a possible.'

'Probable?'

The line went dead. Officious bastard, Ryder thought as he hung up the phone and left the drugstore. Still, speed was everything with these temporary phone-drops. Not too much information was given out in any one week, but the number was changed the next week anyway. Honey's phone stayed the same throughout. She would sound like a pretty popular girl to anybody tapping her.

He returned to the Waldorf, took the Tower elevator to his suite and let himself inside. Everything seemed to be in place, except for the dinner things, which had disappeared.

Moving methodically, Ryder checked the layout of the living room and bathroom, and ended up in the bedroom. He opened the bureau drawers and examined their contents. He was willing to take a Bible oath that they had not been searched.

Pulling both drawers out of the bureau, he examined the tattletales and found that both had turned black on the sensitive spot. The chemical in them was arranged so that, when the drawer was opened, the tape separated, exposing the sensitive spot to air. Within ninety seconds, the chemical turned black.

Ryder sat down on the edge of the bed and evaluated the situation. Peter was a good man, damned good. And behind Peter stood something a lot cannier than the Sovint people, something that had moved Peter into play sixteen months before, almost half a year ahead of Ryder's move to Chicago.

Where did Peter stand now? Having found the room clean, would he cross Ryder off the list? Or was his operation broad enough to be able to check Ryder all the way back to Chicago and the cover he had used there, under the Henderson name? If so, were Peter's folks good enough to penetrate the cover? Having penetrated it, how would they evaluate the news that Henderson was one of Schroeder's people?

But it would never come to that, Ryder told himself as he lay back on the bed and stared at the light green ceiling. Even if they had a Chicago function, the cover was just too solid to be broken.

But what, he asked himself, if there had been a tail on Craigie? That business with the cigar-band had been Craigie's own improvisation, the stupid gesture of a stupid man. And it was enough to tie him to Ryder.

CHAPTER EIGHT

Dressed for sleep, Ryder lay under the light summer blanket and tried to do the final analytical job the Colonel always demanded on the eve of a conclusion.

Now, with the operation rolling to its predestined end, a final analysis tested the weak links, the appearances, the probabilities, the possibilities, everything that could lead, tomorrow afternoon, to success and only that.

'We have absolutely no allowable margin for error,' Schroeder's warning returned to him now in the darkened room. Ryder felt his heart slow for one dragging beat, then resume its normal tempo.

Well, he told himself, the Colonel had nothing to complain about this time around. Everything had gone according to pre-op strategy and, with some small exceptions, the Colonel could give himself a pat on the back.

'You have probably worked out our major problems,' Schroeder had told him at the third briefing almost a year before. This had been a formal affair, complete with Kittredge, the Colonel's second, and a girl operating the tape recorder that scrambled voices according to prearranged sequence memorized by the girl. During the week that followed, Ryder would have the privilege of running and rerunning tapes of the session, as long as the girl was on hand to unscramble them. This final briefing was to be his last contact with Schroeder, since the Colonel had already given far too much time to the operation as it was.

And well he might, Ryder thought somewhat sleepily now as he lay in the darkened room. He sighed and became aware of the bed beneath him, firm but comfortable. Recognizing the first symptom of oncoming sleep, he lighted a cigarette and watched its glow in the darkness as he continued his final analysis.

'We are almost one hundred per cent certain,' Colonel Schroeder had said at the final session almost a year ago, 'that if New York is chosen, there will be an assassination attempt on K. The opportunity is much too good to pass up.' He had paused and glanced at Kittredge, then back at Ryder. 'Do you agree?'

Ryder had shrugged. 'How would you go about liquidating him?'

Schroeder nodded to Kittredge, who began talking almost instantly. 'The day he arrives in New York. Not at Idlewild, because it's too open and everyone's keyed up to an unusual pitch of awareness. Not,' he went on eagerly, 'during the motorcade to Manhattan, because every square foot of it will be blocked off and patrolled like no stretch of real estate in the history of mankind. The same holds true for Manhattan itself. They'll come in on the Triboro Bridge, down the East River Drive, past the UN building for a salute and some ceremonies, then reverse direction and head up First to Forty-seventh, across to Park and up to the Waldorf for a triumphant arrival at the main entrance. Every inch of the way under surveillance, vehicles moving most of the time. You see?' He turned his hands palms up, 'Impossible.'

There was a moment of silence. Ryder heard the girl adjust the recording scrambler to a new combination. 'Not quite impossible,' Ryder said then. 'It's true that K has been moving from the moment he hit Idlewild. He would have stepped out into the UN plaza for a moment, but it's wide open and rotten cover for an assassin. But when that motorcade stops in front of the Waldorf he has to get out of the car on his own two legs, walk along under the canopy, and into the lobby. That's when a grenade, dropped from one of the hundreds of windows above, would blow up the canopy, the guards, and K.'

Schroeder poked his pipe into Ryder's shoulder. 'How would we be sure the grenade exploded on time? Too soon and it harms no one. Too late, and some Sovint guard may fall on it and take the blast himself.'

Ryder smiled. 'You're playing games now. A high school boy with a sharp pencil can figure it out. A Mills bomb can be set for any detonation interval from one to seven seconds. Once you've picked your room and made sure it's a clean house, you work out the rate of descent for that height, set the detonation interval, and you're home free.'

'Ah, but can you rely on the mechansim?'

'If our bunch makes it, yes.' Ryder paused. 'You can also cover all bets by releasing two of them simultaneously. You pull the rings and hold back the detonators, one in each hand. As K steps from the car, you just open both hands and plug your ears.'

'But how can you be sure of getting the right room?'

'As long as it's in a vertical line above the entrance, you have about sixteen floors from which to choose.'

'And if none of the rooms are available?'

'You can be off the vertical axis as much as twenty feet. These Mills bombs scatter shrapnel in a burst area with a twenty-five-foot radius.'

'What if Sovint's rented all the rooms on the Park Avenue side?' Kittredge asked.

'Impossible,' Ryder retorted. 'The Waldorf has too many long-time regular guests. They'd never inconvenience them, especially for Sovint.'

Schroeder sat back and nodded. 'Not a bad little plan.'

'Thank you,' Ryder said.

'Oh, it isn't your plan exclusively. Kittredge worked it out a month ago. Except that he was using an impact detonator. Much more reliable than a timing device.'

'Explodes when it hits the sidewalk?'

Ryder asked. 'What more could anyone ask?'

Schroeder shook his head. 'Just a bit more. Kittredge is calling for a "Bouncing Betty" kind of device. When it hits the pavement, a secondary charge pops it up in the air about six feet. Then it blows.'

'Maximum lethal effect.' Ryder nodded. 'What about bystanders?'

'Well . . .' Colonel Schroeder rubbed his chin slowly. 'We can't let a few curiosity-hungry New Yorkers—probably a bunch of Jews anyway—interfere with the work of liquidating K.'

Ryder laughed quietly. 'You give me the creeps, Colonel.'

The three of them fell silent and, in the few moments it gave her, the girl switched to another scrambler pattern.

'The only bug in the operation is that they won't have any Bouncing Betty contraption.' Schroeder sighed. 'So you were probably right, Ryder. It'll have to be a grenade.'

Ryder leaned forward. 'How do you evaluate them, Colonel?'

The older man looked at Kittredge, who stood up and began pacing the fairly small room. Although the Colonel's people did keep files, with folders that could be brought to the meeting, Kittredge believed in leadership by example, Ryder noted. The man was going to quote from memory, impressing Ryder with the usual necessity of following the example.

'We've narrowed them down to two groups. There are a good twenty more organizations that haven't the energy, intelligence, or money to pull off a successful operation of this magnitude. But two groups do. Yours is based in Chicago.'

Ryder squinted for a moment. 'United Sons of America?' he asked. 'Walt Connell's outfit?'

Kittredge nodded. 'Backed by several of the Hungerford millions.'

'What's the other bunch?' Ryder asked.

'The Memphis group around Howard and Paul Caxton.'

'I can't be in two places at . . .'

'Someone else will have the privilege of joining the Caxtons,' the Colonel interrupted. 'Your work for the next year is pretty well cut out for you.'

'Join the Sons,' Ryder said, 'work my way up and . . .'

There was a moment of silence. 'And,' Colonel Schroeder finished for him, 'abort the assassination.'

CHAPTER NINE

Ryder swung his legs off the bed and stubbed out the cigarette. His desire to sleep had been killed. He padded, barefoot, through the rooms of the suite, turning lights on and off, inspecting windows, doing meaningless things he knew meant nothing.

A year, he kept thinking, a year to worm my way in and work my way up.

And yet, in a year, he hadn't quite made it. Neither he nor Craigie was the man tapped for the glorious assignment. The right to drop that historic grenade had been retained by Walt Connell himself, on the good chance that he would be caught and brought to trial. Craigie would have made a poor martyr on the witness stand. Ryder himself was too new to be handed the starring role of ideological spokesman. But with Connell on the stand, fighting for his life, the Sons would enjoy a coast-to-coast recruiting pitch carried in every newspaper and on every television station.

That wasn't Connell's full reasoning. He had also convinced the Council that his trial for murder could move the entire nation to action. More important, he had convinced Old Man Hungerford himself, past eighty, a dried-up, semi-paralysed little horror who had long ago retired from the industrial empire that bore his name.

Ryder returned to his bed and lay down again. But even that, he mused, wasn't Walt Connell's real reason. It lay within the man himself, within the core of shrewdness that had turned an unsuccessful lawyer into the head of a powerful organization. It lay within Connell's own view of himself and his destiny, the personal image of Walt Connell's face on the front page of every newspaper and magazine, in every newsreel, on television—somebody famous at last, someone to reckon with, someone to fear and respect and, perhaps, honor. Someone, in any event, whose name would certainly go down in the history books.

Closing his eyes, Ryder summoned up Connell's own vision of the future, delivered one night at dinner in a private room at Henrici's.

'I'll be sitting there at the defendant's table, Johnny,' he told Ryder. 'The cameras will be trained on me. The microphones will be picking up every word I say. And the jury will file in.

'"Have you reached a verdict?" the judge will say.

'"We have, Your Honor," the foreman will say.

'There'll be a little pause and a rustling of papers on the bench. The judge will clear his throat. "How say you? Guilty or not guilty?"

'"We find the defendant guilty as charged," the foreman will say.

'There'll be a tumult in the court. A tumult and a whispering and a humming. And the judge will pound that gavel and the bailiffs will quiet the crowd. And the judge will look at me. "Walter Bartley Connell," he'll say, "have you anything to say before sentence is passed?"

'And I'll get to my feet. The cameras will be grinding away. The lights will be shining down on my head, Johnny, on me and me alone.

'"Your Honor," I'll say, "I have."

'And I'll step out from behind the table and turn to the cameras, face them full and I'll raise my arm and point my finger right into the lenses.

89

'"Just this, Your Honor. May it please the court, I have three hundred thousand armed patriots in twenty cities of the nation, Your Honor," I'll raise my arm over my head. "And if the people of this glorious land cannot take the law into their own hands, Your Honor, my patriots will show them the way!" And then...'

The intricacies of Connell's personal vision of revolution began to swim and merge together in Ryder's mind as he lay there remembering the past. Kittredge had been wrong on only one little point. The Sons had energy and money, true enough. But aside from Walt Connell, there wasn't enough brain among them to go around. Connell, with the tight rein he kept on his fanatic ambition, was by far the most dangerous of them all. He had a first-class brain, a good grasp of the possibilities of a situation and a fine ability to project probabilities. Ryder had often found himself, in the past year, wishing there were something constructive to be done, some way to channel that mind into useful work.

But the same intelligence that made Connell potentially valuable had created such a sick intensity of arrogance that the man was past usefulness. In the world at large he could never have masked that arrogance enough to get along, to conform to the norms of manners and of 'handling' people.

But it was somewhat of a shame, Ryder thought as he lay there smoking another cigarette, to lose Connell for some useful cause.

Q—What cause would that be?

A—Well . . .

Q—A worthwhile cause for an intelligent man's capabilities should not cause the witness to sink into a stupor.

A—I'll think of the cause. Give me time.

Q—Can it be that the witness has run out of causes?

A—I didn't say th—.

Q—And what about the witness' own cause, to which he has devoted some fifteen years of his life?

A—Well, there's always that.

Q—Would the witness describe in his own words the scope of that cause?

A—I . . . I'm afraid I'm a bit stale. Could the eminent counsel refresh my memory?

Q—This is a court of law, sir, not a quiz show. I ask you a simple question. Name the cause for which you have given fifteen years of furtive, scurrying, nerve-rasping time and energy, for which you have on several occasions given both blood and bits of bone, for which you have been clubbed, kicked, shot at, drugged, seduced and, on one memorable occasion, offered a sizable sum of money—tax free—to betray?

A—You forgot that time I nearly drowned in Lisbon.

Ryder blew invisible smoke into the darkness above him. Odd, he thought, how both he and Connell had those court-room visions. Was it the result of associating too intimately with the man? Was some of Connell's personality rubbing off on him?

Colonel Schroeder would applaud that. It was always desirable to assume protective coloration naturally. The trick was to recognize it as coloration and nothing more.

Ryder put out the cigarette, slid his legs under the light summer blanket and tried to relax his body. That was the trick, he told himself somewhat hazily, to know whose personality was whose.

It was easy, really. You knew who you were and who you weren't. You didn't keep reminding yourself of the differences. No. That confused your day-to-day cover personality. But every once in a while—like now, for example—you sorted out who you were from who you weren't and then you knew who . . .

Ryder found himself running along a corridor of doors, like the temporary sidings they put up around building demolitions. Old doors of varying heights and widths and colors and designs. Light doors with smooth surfaces and sleek handles. Dark oak doors with intricate carved panelling and ornate brass handles.

As he ran he tried a door here and a door there. They were all locked because, as he suddenly reminded himself, they weren't really doors at all, of course, but a kind of barricade to keep out passers-by and sidewalk superintendents who wanted to watch the building being torn down.

But he kept trying the doors because one of them was a real door. It might be a flush door in smooth bleached walnut. It might be a rococo mahogany door with an acanthus-leaf design incised in the rich wood. He kept trying to turn the handles, telling himself that although they were only a mask to hide the demolition behind them, one of them was real.

Through one of those doors he could walk and see the demolition. He could see the building. He could see what had once been a building. He could see the non-building, the anti-building.

A door to the nothing.

He awoke suddenly, covered with perspiration, and wondered for a moment where he was. Placing himself almost at once, he wondered what had awakened him. He wiped his hand over his face and blotted it on the sheet next to him. Had the air conditioning gone off? Was that why he had began perspiring so freely? Was the cessation of its quiet, almost inaudible hum the thing that had awakened him?

He sighed and lay back on the bed, feeling slightly chilly. As he did so, the memory of the dream doors returned to him in a chunk. He could feel perspiration start out on his forehead. No point in returning to sleep just yet, he told himself. He reached for the pack of cigarettes on the bedside table. As he did so, the bedroom lights flared on.

'Lie back,' the waiter said. 'Lie quietly.'

Ryder watched the small eye of the snub-nosed .32 follow his head as it sank back on the pillow.

CHAPTER TEN

In the moment of silence that followed, Ryder sorted out his approaches and his own counter-plays. Another part of him, divorced from the examination of alternatives, was sizing up Peter as an individual man.

He was slightly taller than Ryder had originally thought, possibly a shade more than five-ten, the height previously disguised by a waiter's stoop. He was, if anything, slightly younger now that he stood straighter. Middle to late-middle thirties, with plenty of muscle and all of it in good shape, to judge by the way he moved.

His face was somewhat long, like Ryder's own, a narrowish face with faintly slack cheeks, eyes set a bit wider than normal, grey irises steady around pupils made small by the sudden downpour of light, somewhat bushy eyebrows with a space between them that Ryder believed to be plucked free of hair, a thin-nostriled nose and a fairly wide mouth, the kind that looks friendly.

Peter reached behind him for a light chair, pulled it to within ten feet of the bed and sat down, holding the gun on his knee for support.

'Make yourself comfortable,' he said then without much trace of an accent. 'You have a long wait.'

There were only three alternatives, Ryder had decided. Peter's organization had been able, in the space of a few hours, to check out the Chicago end of things and come up with ... what? Just three things: that Ryder was vaguely suspicious, that under the cover name of Henderson he was an assassin bent on killing K, or that he was one of the Colonel's men. But which? In any event, he had nothing to lose by keeping cover.

'What in hell *is* this, Pete? God's sake, what's that gun for, anyway?'

Peter's wide mouth quirked at one corner. 'Perhaps you'd like to tell me?'

'I'd love to, Pete, but you have me at a disadvantage, as the fella says.'

Peter shook his head. 'Have you examined the gun carefully?' he asked then. He held it sideways for a moment. 'Familiar?' he asked, levelling it at Ryder again.

Ryder frowned. 'Honest, Pete, I don't know what you're gabbing about.'

'It's a brand new, short-barrelled .32 calibre, seven-shot Smith and Wesson revolver with a hair-trigger action,' Peter said quickly, as if reeling off a catalog description. 'I believe the police call it a "belly gun." It's never been fired. At any rate, you have by now recognized it.'

'Search me, buddy.'

'It belongs to a man named Frank R. Craigie, who registered this evening in room 1106 under the name of Frederick Coombs.'

'Is that supposed to mean something to me?'

'Really, Mr. Rutherford,' Peter retorted, 'this sort of thing only wastes your time. I have plenty to waste, of course. You do not.'

Ryder tried to determine whether Craigie had talked. The man was capable of spilling his insides, under the proper pressure, but it was also possible that under the constrained hotel circumstances, Sovint hadn't wanted to take the chance of applying proper pressure. In which case, Peter was on a simple fishing expedition.

'Frank Craigie?' Ryder asked. He shifted

on the bed, more to test Peter's surveillance than to ease his muscles.

The muzzle of the gun followed his body as though homed in on it by radar. 'Craigie?' he repeated. 'I knew a fella named Craigie once in Council Bluffs.'

'This is a Chicago Craigie. A very talkative kind of Craigie, indeed.' Peter's mouth quirked up at both corners this time. 'He fell apart after only the most preliminary kind of interrogation. Hardly more than just talk. But talk he did.'

'If he said anything about me, now, it's a damned lie and you know it.'

'He said so many things.' Peter sighed and paused, as if to shift through the tons of information that had come spilling out of Craigie's mouth. 'He said that he had been sent to New York to assassinate a certain individual, or rather, I should say, to impersonate an assassin. His was the feint. The real blow was to come from another quarter and another man. John Rutherford, in fact.'

'I never heard of anything so preposterous in my whole, entire life,' Ryder burst out. He continued his protestations, working out as well as he could what plan he had to follow now.

It had been the Colonel's thought all along that if K's assassin were to fall into Sovint's hands the net effect could be almost as bad as a successful assassination. At that time, a year ago, they had all assumed that Ryder would be the man in question and that, if nabbed by Sovint, his first duty was to escape and lose himself. No propaganda could be made of an alleged attempt on K's life if Sovint failed to produce a would-be assassin. Now they had two: Craigie and Ryder. What was worse, Ryder reflected, was that they didn't have Connell, the man who would drop the grenade. Worst of all, they were immobilizing Ryder, the man whose mission was to stop Connell at the last moment. By holding Ryder, Sovint was guaranteeing K's death.

Ryder found himself wondering if Craigie had really implicated him at all, or if Peter were running a bluff. Even in panic, Craigie couldn't have given them a man named Rutherford because he knew Ryder only under his cover name of Henderson. It smelled very much like a bluff, standard procedure, for milking information.

'... You're quite finished,' Peter was

saying, 'perhaps we can end this little farce and get down to the facts.'

Ryder shrugged. 'What made you check on Craigie?'

Peter's eyebrows went up slightly. 'You amaze me. Craigie has been known to us for many years.'

'But why take him apart? Why not catch him in the act tomorrow afternoon? Why not ring in the Waldorf cops? What headlines!'

Peter inclined his head for a moment, as if granting the possibilities of the idea. 'It was not my assignment,' he said then. 'And, in any event, it would seem plain enough to anyone that Craigie could not be depended upon to do his job alone.'

Ryder started to reach for a cigarette. 'May I?'

'Certainly.' Peter watched him light up. 'And now, Mr. Rutherford, we can proceed.'

Ryder explored the areas of information Peter might want. If they had had Craigie pegged, it was inconceivable that they could ignore the possibility of Connell. They would want to know when, where, under what name, what possible disguise, everything about Connell's arrival. But the timetable would run off too fast for them. At one-forty-five tomorrow afternoon, as K's motorcade was leaving the UN building, Connell would enter the Waldorf sub-basement through a door from a private New York Central siding. He would be dressed as a Waldorf maintenance man. At one-fifty-five, while Connell worked his way toward the Tower, using service elevators, Ryder would see the motorcade turn the corner at Forty-seventh Street and proceed up Park. He would call the desk and complain that two of his lights weren't working. The Sovint tap would relay this information to its boys watching the corridor. They would be prepared, then, for the sight of Connell hurrying to Ryder's room, bearing a cardboard pack of light bulbs. By two o'clock, when the motorcade halted at the main entrance below Ryder's window, Connell would be ready for his supreme act. Ryder would slug him, wash a heavy dose of Seconal down his throat, bind him, and stuff him in a closet. He would keep Connell drugged and fed for the next three days until, the summit meetings over, he could leave Connell to be found by the cleaning crew. He would do exactly what Peter would now do to Ryder.

'All right,' Ryder said, maintaining his Midwest accent, but dropping the Babbitt verbiage, 'what now?'

'It's for you to say, Mr. Rutherford. And you have a great deal to say, don't you?'

Ryder blew a plume of smoke into the air and reflected that smoking in the light seemed more satisfying than smoking in the dark. 'I knew I'd made a mistake, giving you such a small tip.'

This time Peter actually laughed, although the movement did not affect the steadiness of his gun hand. 'Two dimes,' he said. 'Really, Mr. Rutherford.'

In addition to recognizing Peter's bluff, another bit of information made Ryder's position somewhat easier to evaluate. Peter was apparently handling this alone, which seemed to argue that Sovint wasn't actually working on this particular problem. Their standard technique was a massive show of force within the first thirty seconds, a whirlwind of lights, men, orders, shoving around, guns in the ribs, all designed to throw the suspect off center and start him wobbling eccentrically. But Peter seemed perfectly willing to digress for a moment or two, showed no sign of getting ugly, and worked his suspect alone.

Ryder reminded himself that Peter had been planted in cover here some sixteen months ago. His lack of any real accent pointed to special training or background far beyond the usual Sovint man, who was simply a very highly-paid and strictly-disciplined cop. The thought struck Ryder as he watched the other man, that he was possibly face-to-face with his own opposite number.

Somewhere in Russia there was another Colonel Schroeder and another special group.

'I've given you more than enough time,' Peter said then, 'to work out a clever story accounting for Mr. Connell's whereabouts and itinerary.' He paused and sighed softly. 'Supposing we dispense with it completely. It's undignified for us to waste our time on impromptu performances. We can, if nothing else, remain intelligent men.'

'In other words, you want his true itinerary?'

'In other words, yes.'

'And if I won't give it to you, Peter?'

Watching the man gather himself together in a more compact posture, Ryder tried to evaluate his chances of outwitting or overpowering this man. Because if Peter kept him here under a gun or took him away—it didn't much matter which—then Connell would be forced to improvise tomorrow. And, because Connell was a dangerously bright man, K would be dead by five-past-two.

'What will you do then, Peter?'

Peter stood up. Keeping the gun trained on Ryder, he went to the window and opened it several feet. 'Knock you out,' he said, one corner of his wide mouth turning upward in a friendly grin, 'shove you out of the window and compose the saddening suicide note of an assassin who lost his nerve.'

CHAPTER ELEVEN

Moving slowly, Ryder sat up in bed and swung his legs over the side. Physically, he told himself, Peter had the upper hand. He had the gun, true, but more important in an interchange of lies like this one, he was fully clothed, whereas Ryder had on only his underwear shorts. From long experience in this kind of colloquy, Ryder knew the importance of physical superiority. He slid slowly off the bed and stood up.

'May I put on my robe?'

Peter shook his head, breaking into a full-fledged between-us-boys smile. 'Let us leave it as is,' he said. 'What do they call it in England? One up?' He nodded, pleased with the idea. 'I shall remain one up. Sit back on the bed, if you please.'

Ryder could feel the psychological balance swing back inexorably toward Peter. The fact that Peter might be bluffing didn't help a great deal. It was good enough, as far as it went, but it still didn't give Ryder any psychological leverage. What he needed, he decided, was a good, fast outburst.

'Like hell I will!' he burst out in a loud voice.

Peter blinked and took a step toward him, gun levelled at Ryder's abdomen. 'Lower your voice, Mr. Rutherford.'

'The hell I will!' Ryder exclaimed. 'Now, get this straight, you, whatever your name is. I've been peaceful and easy-going long enough. Trouble with you is, when you see a man's good-natured, you itch to walk all over him. Well . . .' he filled his lungs and shouted his next words, 'you're not walking all over *this* cookie, nosiree! Just try it and see how wrong you can be!'

The gun muzzle jerked sideways. 'Quiet!'

'Nuts!' Ryder retorted, opening his eyes wide and working up a kind of breathless, choked quality to his voice. 'Just get a few things straight in that knotty head of yours. I never heard of anybody named Craigie. Paste it in your hat, boy. Craigie means nothing to me! Secondly, because I never heard of him and you know it, you're trying to run some sort of bluff with me. What it's all about,' he went on, speeding up the tempo of his words and running thoughts together in headlong haste, 'I don't know and couldn't care less, but I'll tell you this, buddy-boy, one thing I do know and that is you'll end up in the looney-bin sooner than you expected if you go around waking people up and shoving a gun in their faces and threatening to throw them out windows and screaming all kinds of insane nonsense about assassinations and garbage like that!'

He stopped, really out of breath, and exaggerated the way he was panting to regain his wind, confident that Peter, wanting him alive to give information, would let him yell his head off. The moment he saw Peter's mouth twist slightly to speak, Ryder began shouting again.

'And another thing, buddy, if you're so goddamned, all-fired smart, why the hell don't you learn to do your job right? I never heard of a sneak-thief crazy enough to work the Waldorf, but if he was—and you must be—the first thing he'd do is go through a man's wallet. Well, *there* it is! There it *is*!' Ryder's finger trembled as he pointed at the dresser top. '*Look* at it! *See* it? What's stopping you? Lift it up! What's the matter, afraid to? Go ahead, open it! Look inside! You'll see who I am. It's all there, every bit of it. Go ahead, look at it!'

Peter's eyes shifted a fraction of an inch, merely to confirm the wallet's existence, and then shifted quickly back to Ryder. 'Mr. Ru—.'

'I'll tell you one thing sure,' Ryder burst out suddenly, pleased at the hoarse note that had crept into his voice, 'if I ever get out of this alive, I'm going to take all the time and money it needs to put you behind the bars of an insane asylum! That's where you belong, too, goddamn it! Now, will you put that silly gun away and get the hell out of here? Go on, now. Beat it!'

The room was suddenly, almost painfully, silent to Ryder's ears, after the intensity of passion with which he had filled it. He glanced down at Peter's gun, breathed heavily for a few moments more and then reached abruptly for a cigarette.

The snap of the match as he struck it sounded too loud in the quiet room. He applied the flame to the cigarette, not trusting himself to look at Peter. The man's silence was encouraging. Perhaps he had succeeded after all, not in convincing Peter of his innocence, but in shaking Peter's bluff. The longer he remained silent, the better chances were.

Moving with the kind of off-tempo muscular jerks that come from tremendous inner tension—Ryder had worked up a variety of these tics, for both his hands and his face—he strode to the dresser, picked up the wallet and whirled to face Peter.

'Well?'

Peter's forehead creased very slightly. He sat down on the window seat. 'Well,' he echoed. 'All in good time, Mr. Rutherford.'

'The hell with that!' Ryder retorted. 'I want you to look through it right now. I don't want you cluttering up this suite any more. And if you think you've got a job left with the Waldorf after tonight, brother, you're loonier than you act.'

Peter seemed to think about this for a long moment, although Ryder understood that he was really thinking of the previous gambit, the outraged innocence routine. As soon as Peter spoke, Ryder realized why the gambit had apparently worked.

'I did not personally interrogate Craigie,' Peter admitted. 'He was apprehended by the hotel police. It is possible that he did not implicate you by name. But his actions implicated you as strongly as if he had named you.'

'Implicated me in what?' Ryder barked. 'This silly assassination scheme of yours?' He paused, struck by a good thought. 'Just who are you going to assassinate?' he pounced then.

'Please, Mr. Rutherford, things are becoming confused enough as it is.'

'Didn't you say ...?' Ryder stopped himself, sensing that his thought didn't need to be pounded home any further. 'Anyway, how did this Craigie implicate me? How in hell did you ever get into my hair in the first place? That's what I'd like

109

to know.'

Peter shrugged, although the gun remained steady. 'In the lobby, earlier this evening, he dropped a cigar-band at your feet.' The minute the words were out of his mouth, his face grew very slightly darker, as though even he realized how inane his words sounded.

'*What?*' Ryder exploded.

He pulled in a great gasp of air. '*What?*' he bellowed again. 'Are you out of your loving mind, man? Are you stark raving mad?'

'I must ask you to keep your voice...'

'Cigar-bands!' Ryder thundered. 'My God! Cigar-bands! I ask you,' he raved on, appealing to the four walls as his witness, 'I ask you have you ever heard of such a stupid, ridiculous....'

From the living room came the sudden sound of pounding on the door. Ryder broke off and stared in the direction of the noise. Moving quickly Peter stepped behind the bedroom door and gestured with the revolver. 'Answer it and say nothing. This will be trained on you all the time.'

Ryder padded on bare feet into the living room. Hand on the knob, he saw the muzzle of Peter's gun poke out at him between the bedroom door and jamb. He opened the front door and looked at two men he had never seen before.

The taller of the two, with a neck as beefy as a steer, stood behind the shorter one, who had prepared a sugary smile. 'I'm sorry, sir,' he said. 'Is everything all right?'

Ryder stepped back, inviting them in without saying so. They took the hint. 'Who are you?' he asked the smaller man.

'I'm the house man, sir. This gentleman here,' he indicated the beefy one, 'heard shouting and wondered if, well...'

'Shouting?' Ryder asked.

Out of the corner of his eye he could see the gun muzzle disappear. A moment later the bedroom door swung open. 'What is it?' Peter asked, coming out into the living room. There was no sign of a gun.

Ryder watched a glance pass between Peter and the bullnecked man. In Peter's look there was a faint questioning. In the beefy one's eyes lay a too-stony lack of recognition. Nevertheless, Ryder reminded himself, Peter didn't come out of cover until he saw the big fellow.

'Is this ... isn't this ...?' The house detective was having trouble recognizing

Peter without his waiter's uniform, but he finally identified him. 'You're Voynow, aren't you?'

'I am. Yes.'

'What are you doing in here out of uniform?'

'Has he been causing trouble?' the beefy one asked suddenly in a Sovint accent, Ryder told himself, as thick as sour cream.

'What's been going on, sir?' the house man asked Ryder.

'Damned if I know,' Ryder replied. 'He came bursting in here waving a gun and yelling all kinds of crazy accusations.'

'What accusations?' the beefy man asked.

Thinking that it would have been more polite to leave the question to the house detective, Ryder chose a direction slightly more neutral than the ones open to him. 'I can't make heads or tails of it,' he said. 'Maybe you can get it out of him. I can't. And what's more I don't want to. All I want is some sleep.'

'Quite right, sir,' the house detective agreed. He grabbed Peter's arm. 'Let's step along, Voynow.'

'He's got a gun,' Ryder couldn't resist adding. Before the house man could move, the beefy man's hands flickered up and down Peter with the agility of butterflies, located the revolver and removed it. Then, almost as an afterthought, the weapon was handed over to the house detective.

'I'll see that you aren't disturbed any more tonight, sir,' the house man assured Ryder.

The last thing Ryder saw as the three of them left his suite was Peter's wide-set grey eyes, turned on him with a long, remembering glance.

After he had gotten back in bed, Ryder tried to work out what had gone wrong with Sovint, what wires had crossed. He could understand Sovint calling Peter off because he was barking up the wrong tree. But they would do it very privately and they'd keep the hotel police far out of it. What had happened just now looked almost as though someone at Sovint was being purposefully vindictive . . . toward Peter.

In any event, and regardless of what it all meant, one thing was clear: the suite was no longer a clean house. That meant another plan had to be worked out, another room used to hold Connell under wraps until after the summit meeting.

The best thing, Ryder decided as he lay

back courting sleep again, would be to use one of the rented but unoccupied suites on the eleventh or sixteenth floors. He had a mental list of such suites, any one of which would do. He would have to picklock his way in and set himself up without the downstairs clerks getting wind of it. The floor personnel mustn't know, either. And, some way, he had to get word to Connell that the original suite was too hot to use. Otherwise, the plan would work just as designed, even with the room change.

Lying in the darkness, feeling sleep surround him, Ryder's mind worked its way back to what had fouled up within Sovint. He thought about the beefy man and the truculent who-the-hell-do-you-think-you-are look he had privately given Peter. He thought for a while of Peter's questioning glance.

Poor Peter. And just when Ryder was getting to like him.

CHAPTER TWELVE

Ryder's first thought, as he lay quietly, hoping for sleep, was that anyone else

Connell might have assigned to this job would never have stood up to an operative as professional as Peter.

Anyone else of Connell's people would long ago have been immobilized. It was a mark of Connell's peculiar mind that he could not anticipate the sort of sophisticated trouble Peter represented. For that matter, he could not envision the even more involved trouble represented by Ryder.

Ryder wondered again, as he had so often in the past, how much of Connell's success was due to basic intelligence and how much to insane luck. He wondered about it from the very beginning, from the first time he'd met Connell a year before.

Ryder had taken on, along with his Henderson personality, a Newspaper Guild membership card and a background of journeyman newspaper work, none of which could be checked except for a specific San Fransico reference Colonel Schroeder's people were prepared to back up as true. Schroeder had left to Ryder the details of meeting Connell and ingratiating himself. 'As a newspaperman,' the Colonel had said, 'you can make the meeting natural enough. From then on, play it by ear but play it fast.'

Ryder had finished his first month as a reporter-re-write man on a neighborhood newspaper in Chicago when Connell staged a mass, open-air rally on the far Southwest Side. Ryder reported the meeting accurately but unsympathetically, citing several instances of poor organizational technique. 'One observer,' his story concluded, 'pointed out that a group hoping to reorganize the nation in its own image would do well to begin organizing its own efforts more efficiently.'

The next day Connell sent two of his cretin muscle men around to invite Ryder to talk. Their mission had been peaceful enough but Ryder deliberately mistook their intent. He left both men in the gutter outside the newspaper office, one with a sprained wrist, the other with a knob behind his left ear the size of a small, but probably very bitter, lemon.

The image Ryder thus projected proved irresistible to Connell. In retrospect, Ryder knew now, he could not have picked a better way to bring himself to Connell's attention.

Ryder had been sipping a beer at a bar near the newspaper when Connell came in the door with the same two unsuccessful plug-uglies he had sent before. The heavy-set man eased himself into the stool next to Ryder while his guards took up positions near the door with the self-consciousness of amateurs remembering a gangster film.

'I hear,' Connell began without preamble, 'that you could organize the Sons of America a hell of a lot better than me.'

That had been the start of the relationship, violent and abrupt. Connell had quickly satisfied himself that Ryder had no glaring political differences with the organization. Within a week, Ryder was on Connell's staff at nearly double his newspaper salary. His job was something purposefully vague in the general area of public relations.

Ryder's early assignments were hack work, speech-writing, brochures, a brief stint to the south organizing cells in the Cairo-Louisville area. Having briefly tested him, Connell recalled him to headquarters in less than a month. He was installed in the fortress Old Man Hungerford had turned over to the Sons as national headquarters and Phase One of Ryder's assignment from Schroeder had been completed.

'You're part of my cadre now, Johnny,' Connell said. 'At HQ we don't futz around. Hard work . . . good pay. As of now you draw three big bills a week. If you work out the way you have been, you'll make more. I take care of my cadre, Johnny. That's why they take care of me.'

The slow work of inching his way closer into Connell's confidence, Ryder found out, went no faster now that he was part of the Headquarters staff. Connell had no Number Two man. He functioned alone with a tremendous gap between himself and his nearest subordinates. Whenever he got the chance Ryder pointed out, as subtly as he could, how dangerously inefficient this form of organization was, what a great burden it placed on Connell, how much more work could be done by delegating authority to trusted lieutenants, and how much better the second echelon would be trained by assuming such responsibility.

Each time he did, however, Connell grew almost sullen in his silence. Finally, one night as the two of them were returning from a rally in Gary, Indiana, Ryder cautiously brought up the point again. Connell had been drinking rather freely from an iced bottle of bourbon he kept in a tiny refrigerator bar behind the chauffeur's seat.

'Knock it off, Johnny,' he growled. 'Lieutenants are dangerous. And you don't make me at all happy harping on the same goddamned string.'

'Forget it, Walt,' Ryder said quickly.

Connell brooded for a moment. 'Lenin had lieutenants. Hitler, too. What good did any of 'em do?'

'How can you compare yourself to men like that?' Ryder asked. 'You can't even compare this country to Russia or Germany. We're a different breed. The Russians and Germans don't fight authority. A Number One Boss makes sense to them. But Americans are the exact opposite. We're committee-lovers. You can put over almost anything if you have a committee do it.'

Connell laughed quietly for a long moment. Then, his heavy face growing grave, he tapped Ryder's knee with a thick finger. 'Y'just said something deep, Johnny-boy,' he intoned solemnly. 'Y'just showed me y'got a hell of a better head on your shoulders than I ever suspected.'

'Is that a compliment?'

'Meant it for one. I knew you were bright. But, the woods are full of bright boys.' Connell prodded his knee harder now, ramming his thick finger insistently against the thin skin over the bone. 'What you said showed me you know the score, part of it, anyway. If you knew the whole score, Johnny, I'd have to dump you like a ton of garbage.'

'What part don't I know?'

'Never mind, bright boy. Point is, the number of people I've found who know as much of the score as you, who really know a little about what makes people tick, I can count on the fingers of one lousy hand.'

Ryder sat back in the rear seat of the limousine and said nothing for a moment. Then: 'You know a lot more about human nature than you let on, Walt.'

'Damned right I do,' Connell agreed. 'That thing you said about power, about the difference between the Germans and us. You and I know there's no difference anywhere in the world, huh, boy? It's just in the appearance of it. We know everybody looks for a boss. Everybody wants a boss. Look at you. Independent, fearless newspaperman. But you want a collar and a leash, too, huh, boy? It's human nature to submit. The only thing about Americans is, you have to con them into submitting by making it look as if they're still their own boss. Give them a lie to believe and they follow like peaceable sheep. Am I right?'

'You remember Huey Long?' Ryder asked suddenly.

'Remember him?' Connell laughed. 'There isn't anything about that man I'm likely to forget.'

'Remember what he said about fascism in this country?'

Connell's face grew solemn again. 'We'll have fascism here,' he quoted slowly. 'Only we'll call it anti-fascism.'

Ryder nodded. 'He knew the score, too.'

'Part of it, Johnny, only part of it. Otherwise he wouldn't've ended up as a worm dinner.' Connell hunched his big frame closer to Ryder. 'Now listen,' he said, lowering his voice on the off chance that the driver could hear him. 'Listen hard, Johnny. I'm going to tell you something I never told another soul. Not even Old Man Hungerford, the silly bastard.'

'Silly, rich bastard,' Ryder amended.

Connell smirked. The street lights, as the

car passed by them, cast changing shadows on his beefy face, making the thick cheeks and heavy chins flicker peculiarly, as if writhing with a private kind of glee. The car was speeding north now along the Outer Drive past the Planetarium and the Band Shell in Grant Park. They were nearly home.

'Johnny,' Connell went on, 'these mouth-breathers and turd-kickers I'm lashing together as an organization, they're the natural-born sheep who follow any good, strong hater. The Sons can use all of them I can gather in. But some day I have to strike out for the people I haven't reached yet. They're beginning to know I'm alive and there's something about me that rings a bell inside of them, but they wouldn't be caught dead in the Sons, not yet. They're the fat ones, young fella, all the scared fat slobs who're too panicked to know I'm their Messiah. One day I'll make my move for them. A big show of power, that's the only way with panicky people. Power attracts. Show enough of it and you draw millions of people to it. Not because it makes sense and not because it stands exactly for what they want, but just because it's pure, naked power and they can submit to it.'

Ryder nodded slowly. 'I think I know what you mean, Walt.'

'I doubt it. But you will in time.' Connell's low, urgent voice rumbled in Ryder's ear: 'Power's a flame. Moths don't want to die but they fly right into the heart of it. That second when they're burning up, that last second, it's like ... like being born again.'

Neither of them spoke for a long moment. The skin across Ryder's shoulders crawled for an instant. The car surged up over the bridge and, after a few blocks, turned left and headed down a side street toward the modern white-brick apartment building where Connell lived.

'That's how we're going to get all the fat, scared moths, Johnny,' Connell said softly.

Trained to notice tiny detail, Ryder nearly missed the change in Connell's pronouns. So powerfully had Connell expressed himself that it was not until the car had stopped and the driver opened the rear door that Ryder realized Connell had stopped saying 'I' and had actually said 'we.'

'Come up for a drink,' Connell said, curving his thick arm around Ryder's

shoulder and propelling him toward the
entrance of the building. Then once they
were out of earshot of the driver: 'Laid on a
little party for myself, kid. But there's an
extra whore for you.'

His apartment took up the entire
penthouse, with terraces facing east toward
the lake and south toward the bright lights
of the Loop. The two women were
sprawled on a long, low divan in front of a
fireplace, holding hands.

They had been drinking bourbon from a
bottle that was now three-quarters empty.
Although he was fascinated by what was
happening. Ryder's eye automatically
noted the torn scrap of revenue stamp on
the floor that told him the bottle had been
opened that evening. The women were
probably quite drunk.

The tall, husky blonde smiled coldly as
Connell introduced her. She got to her feet
and turned her strange, menacing smile on
Connell, stroking her great breasts as she
did so. Although he was well over six feet in
height, the blonde in her high heels was as
tall as he. The brunette, smaller, seemed
vaguely troubled and, in some way Ryder
didn't understand, hurt.

'Are you and me ...?' She paused in

mid-question. Ryder got the idea that she would rather have what was left of Connell after he finished with the big-breasted blonde. He shrugged and poured himself a drink. Then he handed the bottle to the brunette. 'We can always while away the time with this,' he suggested.

'Don't wait for me, kids,' Connell muttered.

His face had grown heavily flushed by the thick, turgid blood surging through his veins. He was breathing quickly, with an impatient effort and, when he looked into the blonde's small, hard eyes, he moistened his lip. Her muscular arm encircled his waist and began kneading the flesh of one buttock. Then she turned him around and headed him for a bedroom in back. 'Don't forget something,' she said then. Connell stopped, opened the drawer of a cabinet and drew from it a short, very flexible riding crop. 'Come on,' the blonde said urgently. They disappeared into the bedroom.

Ryder swallowed bourbon. After a while, his face composed, he turned to the small brunette. Her face was empty of expression except a kind of mute injury. 'Rather be in there?' Ryder asked.

She nodded. 'I dig that kick.' She watched the closed bedroom door.

'Do you now?'

'Um-hm. You?'

The brunette smiled lazily. Her tiny white teeth were so pointed they seemed triangular. 'Do you?' she persisted. 'Like to find out?'

Ryder watched her. 'Do you come up here often?'

'Twice a week.'

He examined her arms, her rather thin legs and the creamy pallor of the small, soft mounds that rose out of her dress. He found no bruises. I'd never have suspected,' he said then.

Her smile grew sharper around the edges. 'You gonna be up here with Walt from now on?'

'I don't know. Sometimes maybe.'

'Then why not try it on for size?' she offered.

He pulled her in toward him. Her teeth sank into his lower lip. The taste of blood flooded his mouth. He shoved her away and watched her slowly, almost thoughtfully, lick her lips. From the bedroom, through the closed doors, Ryder heard a sharp grunt of pain.

The brunette smiled again, pityingly. 'How'd a square like you hook up with Big Walt?'

For the next half hour they drank and talked fitfully about almost nothing. From the bedroom Ryder could hear muffled moaning and short, hacking sobs. Finally there was a high, almost inhuman screech and then a long silence.

The door opened. The big blonde, face damp with effort, strode from the room, her high heels rapping hard on the floor, her breasts heaving with the effort of her breath. She glanced at the brunette and jerked her chin at the outer door. The brunette picked up her bag and trotted after the big woman. Ryder sat without moving until he heard the outside elevator doors open and close.

Then he got to his feet and moved soundlessly across the heavy pile rug to the open door of the bedroom. He looked at Connell's heavy body, calves and buttocks bulging with thick slabs of muscle.

Connell lay naked, face down on the oversize bed, his head turned sideways, his eyes shut, his mouth gaping into the rumpled sheets. Across his broad back and the tight mounds of his rump a series of hot red welts criss-crossed and twisted like agonized snakes. As Ryder watched, Connell began to snore.

Lying, himself, on another bed now, a year later but remembering so well that night, Ryder thought about Connell's kind of power, Connell's understanding of it.

He closed his eyes, as if to blot out the visions he had conjured up in the bedroom of the Waldorf. Slowly, sleep overtook him.

CHAPTER THIRTEEN

Ryder was taking the catboat on a long tack across the Sound toward Greenwich harbor. The wind was north-east at a good twenty knots and Ryder had put the craft into a long port tack that would bring him to within a half mile of shore about a mile below Greenwich. His starboard reach would then bring him to the mouth of the harbor.

Small, busy white clouds flew low across the sky in squadrons, their apparent motion increased by the small boat's movement in the opposite direction. Ryder kicked off his deck shoes and let one foot trail in the water as it raced by a few inches below the heeling port gunwale. The shift in weight started the craft heeling even more to port and Ryder scrambled quickly to starboard, wondering how he had ever gotten dreamy enough to pull a boner like that.

Someone in another boat—a Lightning by the look of her—was gaining fast on Ryder off his stern. The broad-beamed catboat was no match for the Lightning and in a few minutes it swept by. Ryder waved lazily as it passed.

Although his father had offered to help him buy a Lightning that spring before the war, Ryder had insisted on using his own money, about ninety dollars, to buy the catboat, an eighteen-foot veteran that had needed a new mast and very probably some rib braces up forward where it had leaked a small but steady amount of water all that summer. It was roomy enough for six people, his friends and Connie's, and a lot faster than it looked. All in all—there being no dry-rot—it had been a good buy.

Ryder yawned and slid down onto the duckboards, stretching out full length in the sun. Behind closed eyelids he could almost see the clouds pass between him and the immense redness of the sun, intervals of greenish darkness that signalled the difference between light and shadow.

When he awoke, the sun had clouded over except for a patch of blue to the south over Long Island. Ryder sat up and checked the shore for points of reference. The bell buoy off his port bow looked like. . . .

After a few minutes of checking meaningless buildings and towers, of trying to remember buoy numbers and getting completely confused, Ryder realized that he was lost. By dead reckoning, his watch told him that he could be anywhere from Greenwich on north-east to Stamford. But if the wind had shifted, the catboat was sensitive enough, without a hard hand on the tiller, to sharpen its tack enough to bring him miles below Greenwich, as far south-west as Port Chester or even Mamaroneck.

Meanwhile, it was spoiling up for some nasty weather. If he could only get his bearings, he might still make a run for Greenwich Cove and enough shelter to ride out the line storm. The wind hadn't shifted its quarter, he noted, which made matters a bit easier to judge.

At that moment the sky over Long Island was shattered by four quick-dipping strokes of lightning. The sound came to Ryder a few moments later and, with the thunder, the first drops of rain. The wind freshened quickly until he gauged it as close to 40 knots. He reefed in a few yards of mainsail, struggling to keep his footing as the boat began digging into and leaping out over the suddenly choppy water.

As he reached out to grasp a handful of jib and pull it down, a wave broke over the bow and washed him back along the short foredeck, scrambling wildly for a brace to cling to. He felt his body thud hard against the centerboard case. A sharp pain shot through his left shoulder.

Wind and rain drove in hard over the bow now. The boat was losing way. Ryder fought back to the stern and jammed the tiller hard starboard, hauling the boom in the same direction in an attempt to heel about enough to pick up an edge of the gale.

The next half hour seemed to blur. He was gasping for breath. The rain drove almost horizontally across him. Unable to use his good arm because he needed it to hold on, Ryder found his bad one almost useless in setting sail or steering. When he was finally at Greenwich Cove he had to fight a wave of near unconsciousness that swept over him.

But the sight of a familiar land conformation gave him enough strength for a final effort. Badly hurt in the left arm, he

131

managed to scrape the catboat up against a sheltered dock and secure enough fenders to keep it from cracking its side against the pilings. He pulled himself up on the dock and looked around him.

His first thought was to call Connie or his parents. They had to know that he was safe. Leaning into the driving wind, he made for a small metal phone box at the end of the dock, got inside and fought the door closed. Water ran down his body and turned the floor of the booth sopping wet before he could get the receiver off its hook.

'Operator?' He jiggled the phone. 'Operator?' His fingers dug into the sodden pockets of his trousers, searching for a coin, any coin, enough to drop in and get the operator's attention. He found a dime finally and, although this was a five-cent call, dropped it in.

'Number, please.'

'Greenwich 3504.'

'I'll give you Long Distance, sir.'

There was a confused clicking and the dime returned to him. 'Long Distance?' He jiggled the hook. 'Operator? Operator?

'Sir?'

'I want Greenwich 3504, not Long Distance.'

'I'm sorry sir; that is a toll call.'

'Operator, Greenwich! Greenwich, Connecticut. It's a nickel call.'

'Not from here, sir. This is Oyster Bay, Long Island.'

Ryder slumped back against the phone booth and stared at the round printed notice that gave the telephone's number. The operator was right. Somehow . . . ?

He stumbled out into the rain and stared wildly around him. Oyster Bay? What had happened to him? Why was he here? How had he come ten or more miles across the Sound, reversed direction completely and ended up in Long Island? How could it . . . ?

Groaning and beginning to shiver now, Ryder came slowly awake in his bed at the Waldorf.

He sat up and reached for a cigarette and matches, wondering why he had dreamed about that day on the Sound again when he hadn't dreamed of it in ten years.

That terrible feeling of not knowing who he was, or why he had ended up where he was, swept over him with the powerful nausea of a hard blow to the pit of the stomach. He rubbed his left shoulder, easing the dream-pain of that day, the dislocation that had taken the rest of the summer to heal.

Why that day of all others, a day in—what?—1940 or 1941?

He struck a match and looked about his darkened bedroom for a moment before lighting the cigarette. For an instant the lost feeling ebbed. Then, as the match went out, it flowed back over him again and he felt a strong urge to strike another match.

What had happened, of course, he had been able to work out after they'd gotten him back home. The doctor who had set his shoulder had been good enough to drive him all the way back to Greenwich. (Good enough, Ryder asked himself now, or just eager for his bill to be paid?) It had been simple enough. The wind had been shifting from northeast to north as he fell asleep. It had continued to shift to northwest and then to west, turning the catboat in a port circle until it was running before the wind toward the opposite shore of the Sound. Nearing Long Island, he had assumed the wind had not shifted, although it had wheeled a good 120 degrees in an hour. And that . . .

Ryder shook his head. It didn't pay to rehash all this old material. It proved nothing and it tended only to confuse him.

And yet, sitting up in bed now, he could not find a way to rid himself of the intense feeling of being lost. That had been, except for the day on the Sound, a pretty good summer. That fall he'd enlisted in the Army. Why did that day still have the power to haunt his dreams?

Was it because that day was his last and sharpest civilian memory? Was it because out of all that had happened in that other life, this was the last letting-go, the final meaning of civilian life that he carried with him into the service and, without a pause, into Colonel Schroeder's group?

Pulling in smoke, Ryder wondered why, at this late date in his life, he had begun to worry about identity. He knew enough about himself to understand that the dream was a memory of lost identity, a terrible moment in rootlessness, a moment when nothing had been what it seemed.

Why did he worry about it now? Was he starting to soften up? Was he beginning to introspect too much? It was a dangerous luxury, with the insidious power to confuse and unnerve. The Colonel had always stressed the danger of it, not only with new people, but again and again with the old pros like Ryder. You never got so experienced that you lost your susceptibility to the inward-searching kind of fruitless hide-and-seek for the person who used to be you.

Ryder had participated in enough of the Colonel's non-operational bull sessions to know that loss of identity was not only a professional tool for a person in his work and a powerful aid in assuming a cover personality, but was also one thing more: When you really lost the person you once were, drowned him in a hundred new identities and accents, cover stories and backgrounds, lived and shook with fear and succeeded and failed with all the new people who were you, it didn't really matter any more what you used to be.

And once it really and truly didn't matter, Ryder mused now, then you were at your most useful, because if it really didn't matter, neither did death.

He took a long pull on his cigarette and sighed out the smoke, worried about his sudden preoccupation with self and motive and death. It was against all the rules. That dream . . .

He heard his front door open and close very quietly.

Sliding out of bed, he was halfway to a

hiding place behind the bedroom's open door when the lights went on. Peter stood there. A line of dried blood slanted downward from one corner of his wide mouth, giving him an atypical grimace. The skin under his left eye looked puffy. In his hand he held a fairly long and dangerously sharp steak knife.

'You look,' Ryder said raising his hands over his head, 'like you could use a shot of vodka.'

CHAPTER FOURTEEN

Peter closed the door of the bedroom behind him and jerked the knife in a gesture that ordered Ryder back onto the bed. He held the blade the way an intelligence man in any country is trained, not point-out like a jabbing instrument, but sideways, blade edge facing the opponent, a slicer on the forward stroke, point driven home on the return. Swords are for puncture wounds; a knife is to slice meat.

'Never say die, eh, Peter?' Ryder asked, sitting on the edge of the bed. 'I'm getting as bored with this as you are.'

'But this time,' Peter said in a conversational tone, as if completing a sentence just uttered, 'the second you raise your voice you will lose the power to speak . . . permanently.'

'The Waldorf will take a dim view of your plans for their steak knife.'

'There is a saying in my country,' Peter began. '"To a tough steak comes a sharp knife." Mr. Rutherford, or whatever your name is, you are a very tough steak. But . . .' He gestured with the blade and smiled pleasantly.

Watching Peter go about the business of propping a chair against the inside of the bedroom door, Ryder reflected that he had met more confusing situations in his time, but no person as contradictory as Peter. Hadn't he been called off? Hadn't the fact that Sovint sicked the house cops on him been enough of a hint? What was going on in that first-class mind of his?

Ryder had to know the answers because K's life hung on his knowing. But as long as Ryder maintained his cover personality, he had no conversational entries to play. Perhaps he was justified in slipping back a notch from the Rutherford cover to the Henderson one. Perhaps he could admit to being Connell's inside man. As long as he refused to be intimidated by the knife, he was safe. Peter needed him alive until he got enough information to stop Connell. It seemed justifiable, then, to break the Rutherford cover and pick up Henderson in order to get a concrete line on Peter.

'That man with the bull neck,' Ryder began in a companionable way. 'Did he give you that eye and lip?'

Peter frowned and settled himself in a chair halfway across the room. 'You have confused our roles,' he said. 'I do the asking now.'

Ryder shrugged. 'It's just that he sounded like he'd be more at home on Nevsky Prospekt than Park Avenue. What's the matter, Peter, did your buddies give you a hard time?'

'Every occupation has its hazards.' Peter crossed his legs and seemed to be getting comfortable. 'As you will shortly find out.'

'Yes, my occupation. That would be assassin, wouldn't it?'

'Neither of us really doubts it.'

'But wasn't there a Connell you kept raving about?' Ryder asked.

'You are a nonentity,' Peter said, smiling slightly as if to assure Ryder that he meant nothing personal. 'Connell, by personality and training, can make the most of an assassination. We expect him, not you, to be the man.'

'We?' Ryder propped his pillow up behind him and lay back in luxurious comfort. 'There's nobody but you, Peter. You seem to be so far ahead of the parade that you can't hear the band.'

'That happens on occasion.'

'It's happened to you, my friend,' Ryder assured him. 'You've got a fat eye and a bloody lip to prove it.'

'I also have my orders, from the highest quarter,' Peter said, 'and the freedom to interpret them as I see fit. I am keeping you wrapped up, Mr. Rutherford, until I sweat out of you the information I must have. It's as simple as that.'

Ryder shook his head. 'Why did the cops release you? I mean, I haven't even been asked to swear out a complaint.'

'They had intended to prevail upon you not to,' Peter said. 'The hotel would have appreciated that very much The publicity ... et cetera.' He grinned at the thought. 'They had been holding me downstairs in a temporary kind of lockup while they waited for morning and a chance to reason with you. The door posed no really serious problems.'

'And once you escaped, you hotfooted it right back to the beefy gent, wanting to know how come and all that,' Ryder said. 'Which is where you collected the bruises. That eye'll be black in another half-hour, you know.'

'Immaterial.' Peter uncrossed his legs and leaned forward. 'We have had our little digression, Mr. Rutherford. Now let us talk of Connell.'

Ryder lighted a cigarette, although he didn't want one, simply to delay long enough to find the right way Henderson would approach his confession. 'You know,' he said at last, 'I've been lying here doing a lot of thinking since they dragged you away. I've been putting two and two together. Now, the beefy lad with the borsht brogue, he sort of tips your mitt. I mean, there's this big international conference here and all this assassination talk. I can be thick, but I'm not stupid. You're some kind of bodyguard for one of the top Russian brass. Right?'

'This is the long way around,' Peter said. 'But if it makes it easier for you . . .'

'Don't rush me,' Ryder insisted. 'Now,

141

then: the hotel cops nab some guy called Craig, who . . .'

'Craigie,' Peter corrected him in a bored tone.

'Craigie, right. Thanks. Now, then, you came running to me because Craigie dropped a cigar-band near me in the lobby, or something. And your idea is that Craigie is a fake, but I'm the real McCoy. Only it isn't me, it's somebody named Connell. How'm I doing?'

'Admirably.'

'You don't know where Connell is or what he's up to, but you figure I do. So you want me to hand him over to you.'

'Or,' Peter added, 'failing that, I can wait here with you until Connell makes contact.'

'Which you can't be sure of.'

'Or,' Peter continued, 'failing that, I can drop you out the window and create a masterful suicide note.'

Ryder frowned. 'How will that save your big boy?'

'It will make it possible for him to cancel the open-car arrival and come in via the underground ramp, as we originally suggested. In the face of this assassination threat, as revealed by your suicide, he can cancel the arrival without losing face.'

'And you people can make propaganda hay out of the suicide.'

'That,' Peter said, 'is not my assignment.' He waited for a moment and then continued. 'On his side, it would be Connell's assignment, of course. He could not resist the propaganda values inherent in the plan, even if he were the apprehended criminal.'

'You seem to know this Connell a lot better than I do, Peter.'

Peter paused again and sighed softly. 'You know,' he said then, 'you must never, under any circumstances, underestimate the intelligence of your opponent. That is a mistake you fanatic amateurs are prone to make. You assume that we know nothing about you because you managed to keep fairly far in the background in Chicago. But we know you, Mr. Rutherford. Or shall I call you John Henderson?'

Ryder ground out his cigarette. 'Just call me John.' He sighed. 'But I do object to that word "fanatic." Do I look like one to you?'

Peter eyed the cigarette on the table. 'May I?' Taking one, he held it idly in his long, powerful fingers, thinking for a while before he spoke again.

'That's what bothers me, Mr. Henderson,' he said at last. 'You don't.'

'Clouded crystal ball?'

Peter shook his head slowly. 'My Chicago reports were too brief,' he said. 'I've asked for more information, but I haven't been anywhere it can reach me discreetly in the last few hours.' He fell silent for a moment. 'It doesn't really matter, of course. Even if I haven't got the information, I have you. The only question is, what have I got?'

'Can I make a suggestion?' Ryder asked.

'By all means.'

Ryder picked up a book of matches and chucked it to the other man. 'If you can lay your hands on fifty-thousand in cash,' he said then, 'you'll get a hell of a good line on me.'

CHAPTER FIFTEEN

Somewhere in the night, church bells rang two o'clock. Ryder stood at the bathroom sink, while Peter watched from the door, and splashed cold water on his face. The agreement had been reached half an hour

144

before. At nine in the morning, Peter would make a phone call. By ten the cash would be delivered. On delivery, Ryder would give him the information.

He had eight hours, Ryder told himself as he dried his face, to take control of the situation, eight hours to outwit or subvert him or, failing that, to overpower and truss him securely until Connell made contact. Taking the towel from his face, he wondered what chance he had of wrapping it quickly around the knife Peter held, and taking him that way.

Peter took two steps back into the bedroom and grinned. 'Finished?'

Or, Ryder mused as he walked back to the bed, he could let it go through and allow Peter to pick up Connell. That would effectively abort the assassination, but it would give them a live criminal to show the world. The Colonel had been clear on that point. No one was to be picked up by Sovint. After K left, Connell was to be released. Keeping him out of Peter's hands was especially important now because, since Craigie was being held by the city police, Sovint had been cheated of the most likely would-be assassin.

That he would eventually take Peter,

Ryder mused, there could be no doubt. Peter knew that a man who suggests a bribe will do nothing to jeopardize getting his money. Therefore, vigilance can be somewhat relaxed.

So thinking, Ryder lay down on the bed. 'I don't suppose Room Service could send up a couple of sandwiches?'

Peter glanced at his watch. 'They'd be happy to.'

'That's right, you used to work here, didn't you?'

'For a long time,' Peter said. 'Pick up the phone, but be very, very careful. I want to keep you alive, Mr. Henderson, but I'm not above cutting you pretty painfully.'

'Can't you call me John?' Ryder asked. He picked up the phone and ordered sandwiches and coffee.

'You know,' Peter said after the phone had been hung up, 'something is still missing in your picture. I get an odd reaction to you.' Peter touched the skin under his eye and winced slightly. 'Are you a man who betrays a comrade for fifty-thousand dollars?' he asked then. 'Are you a man who goes to all this trouble, all this planning, on the off-chance that you will meet someone like me to whom you can peddle information?'

'It was more than an off-chance.'

'Perhaps.'

'No,' Ryder demurred, 'it was a certainty.'

'It seems that way, now, yes. Would it seem that way to you a year ago in Chicago?'

'Nothing surer,' Ryder told him. He cast about for some quick way of getting Peter off the subject. 'You know, I have an odd reaction to you, too. That is, not so much to you, but to that eye and that lip. I get a very odd reaction to the boys who gave you those souvenirs. I wonder why they did it and then I wonder why they let you off so lightly. If they did it at all, why are you still able to walk? Why didn't they just finish the job?'

'You're being paid only to give information.'

'Yes, but a man just has to wonder now and then.' Ryder settled back until he was flat on the bed, and addressed his remarks to the ceiling. 'I have a pretty clear idea of who bullneck is. I think I have you pegged, too. The only thing I don't know is why you lads crossed swords. Or why he let you get away. Or did he? Did you have to

147

escape from your own folks? Now, that's a novel idea.'

He sat up suddenly and stared at Peter. 'Are you really what you seem to be?' he asked.

'But that, my friend,' Peter said in a soft voice, 'was my original question of you.'

'That's no answer.'

'And since you show such brilliance as a deductive reasoner,' Peter went on, 'Perhaps you can find an answer without my help. Just as I,' he added quietly, 'must eventually answer my own question.'

'Nothing hard to figure out about me.'

'No? Let me tell you a few of the things that bother me.' Holding up one hand, Peter touched each finger with the point of the knife as he spoke.

'First, you're not hostile enough for a fanatic. Second, you're too intuitive for an amateur. Third, you have too much intelligence for a common adventurer. There are other things, but these will serve.'

'Common adventurer,' Ryder echoed. 'I don't know if I like that.'

'You weren't meant to,' Peter assured him. 'Is there anything lower in the world than a man who plots and schemes and connives and misleads—for money?'

Neither of them spoke for a long moment. Ryder seemed to feel the vibrations of the question hang in the air between them. Close to the bone, he thought. Pot calling the kettle black.

'People,' Ryder said finally, 'do all sorts of things for money. Some of them will even do it for a cause.'

Peter nodded. 'I've met a great number of people who do things for a cause. Shall we say, hundreds of people and dozens of causes? And of them all, in the end, there were only four who wouldn't sell out their cause for the right price.'

'You must prize the memory of those four.'

'Their cause was not mine. But you're right. I prize their memory.'

'Dead?'

'Why do you ask?' Peter wanted to know.

'I don't know. It's been my experience that people who won't sacrifice their cause in this cold, cruel world of ours generally end up dead.'

'As a matter of fact, I believe these are.'

'But you prize their memory,' Ryder persisted.

'Yes.' Peter was staring at the middle distance and Ryder got a swift insight. He watched his opposite number sitting there, peering into nothing, and realized that Peter was introspecting. Dangerous, on either side of the fence.

'And their cause wasn't yours,' Ryder continued, pushing a step further. 'That's very interesting. Tell me, Peter, what is your cause?'

Slowly, almost unwillingly, Peter's wide-set, grey eyes surrendered their focus on nothingness and looked up into Ryder's eyes. Just as slowly, an awareness of the question flooded the man's face. With it a kind of irritation that Ryder could recognize at once seemed to enter the man's eyes. Ryder understood that irritation perfectly.

'I think,' Peter said in a tight voice, 'we'll have a little silence now.'

Ryder lay back on the bed and watched the ceiling. Peter, he asked himself, what have we here?

CHAPTER SIXTEEN

A faint grey light filtered down onto Park Avenue, making the headlights of an occasional cab seem less bright. Ryder watched this vague pre-dawn sign and slowly let the curtains close over the window. He glanced at his watch. Five-ten.

'You know, Peter,' he said then, not turning around to watch his captor, 'you can't possibly win without me. You understand that.'

Behind him there was silence for such a long moment that Ryder wondered if Peter had fallen asleep on the couch in the living room. As he was about to turn around, however, Peter spoke at last.

'Idle talk,' he said in a small, thoughtful voice.

'No. The odds would be entirely against you.'

'If that is true, my friend, you share the odds.'

'I cheerfully admit that,' Ryder assured him. 'But unfortunately for you,' he added, turning to see Peter, 'although I can tell you what Connell is supposed to do, I can't guarantee that you'll capture him.'

The blank look on the other man's face made Ryder realize suddenly that they had been talking about two different things. He backtracked hastily over their conversation and, before Peter could speak, picked up the thread that had first confused them.

'You see,' he went on hurriedly, 'even in this small matter here today, the larger dilemma is mirrored.'

'Not quite,' Peter demurred. 'In this small matter, as you call it, I am willing to pay for your help. In the larger dilemma, we could never accept help from you.'

Ryder smiled tauntingly. 'The means never did bother you, did it, as long as you could justify the end?'

Peter's wide mouth twisted in a reply that never got said. He looked up at Ryder and then sank back against the couch, looking away. 'I am not political,' he said then in a tired voice. 'In my kind of work, one cannot afford to be political. It is bad for the judgment.'

Ryder thought about it for a moment, about the several administrations under which Colonel Schroeder's group had functioned without the slightest shift in purpose and orientation, about his own feelings—such as they were—and felt an almost overpowering desire to tell Peter who he really was. It was not possible, of course, he told himself at once. As far as Peter was concerned, there was no Colonel Schroeder.

'Nonsense,' he said, finally. 'Twentieth-century man is a political animal. We're all up to our necks in politics.'

Peter's mouth turned down at the corners and his eyes widened in a kind of mocking face. 'You, perhaps,' he granted. 'The terrorist is a political man. That is why so few really talented terrorists exist. The political mind is not realistically oriented.'

'And yet,' Ryder pursued, 'you would refuse my help under normal circumstances.'

'It has not, to my knowledge, been offered,' Peter remarked. 'Are you, perhaps, making an offer?'

'To join you?' Ryder thought for a moment. 'No, you're right. It wouldn't be smart to accept me. I might, in the end, do to you what I'm doing to Connell.'

'That is a part of you that still bothers me,' Peter said. 'If you are so realistically oriented that you can understand the personal usefulness of selling out Connell, why were you so unrealistic as to join him in the beginning?'

'Don't underestimate Connell and his people.'

'They are well financed,' Peter agreed, 'by the most imperialist segments of monopoly capital, but that . . .'

' . . . Has a vaguely political ring,' Ryder cut in.

'Perhaps. One learns to use these verbal shortcuts.'

'And since when does Old Man Hungerford constitute a segment of anything?' Ryder wanted to know. 'He represents a tiny, crackpot fringe of senility made up pretty much of himself and a few others like him.'

'You are being quite unrealistic, I see. Are you not aware,' Peter asked, 'of his connections with several Texas industrialists who subsidize the Caxton group? And of his California friends, as well?'

Ryder shrugged. 'The rich must have their hobbies,' he said in a deliberately light tone. 'Quite a few wealthy people financed some of your groups, in their day.'

Surprisingly, Peter laughed at this.

154

'Hobbies,' he repeated, still laughing, 'how true.'

'But since you're not political,' Ryder went on after a moment, 'none of this should really mean anything to you.'

'It means less than nothing to me,' Peter said, 'except when it threatens the life of someone I must protect. One can argue politics indefinitely, but assassination is murder and there can be no two sides to the question.'

'In war, there are always two sides to killing.'

'Our nations are not at war.'

Ryder sat down at the other end of the couch. 'Wasn't it Lenin who called war the continuation of politics by other means?'

Peter made the same mocking face, eyes wide and mouth downturned, his head rocking from side to side. 'The Devil quotes scripture?' he asked in a teasing way. 'Things have come to a pretty pass.'

Ryder's mind backtracked again, trying to find a small space into which a wedge could be driven. The man had been much too deft to be drawn into political talk, and yet there must be a way.

'I think I see why your superiors gave you that black eye,' Ryder said at last.

'You're unreliable because you're apolitical.'

'My superiors?' Peter asked, his face suddenly deadpan. 'You flatter them.' He got up and walked to the window, keeping his body turned halfway toward Ryder.

'No?' Ryder asked. 'You are reliable? Then you're political.'

'Nonsense!' Peter burst out, obviously irritated at last. 'Tell me, my friend, how could you recognize a political man? You are as apolitical as a stone.'

'That is neither . . .'

'Don't prate of politics, my fine, turncoat friend,' Peter interrupted. 'Your man Connell is political, yes. You have no inner beliefs and we both know it.' He took a breath and tried to calm himself. 'No,' he said then, 'you do have one. You believe in money. I had forgotten.'

'I believe in myself,' Ryder contradicted. 'I believe in money. But first and last, I believe in myself.'

'Really?' Peter stood now with his back to the window, the handle of the steak knife wobbling back and forth in the air as he shook it by its point. 'Is that why you joined the United Sons of America? Do you expect me to believe that a newcomer, an underling like you would be paid that much money? Or,' he went on, 'do you expect me to believe that you joined it in order to sell it out? Either hypothesis leaves me unconvinced.'

Ryder turned his hands palms up. 'Believe what you choose,' he said. 'I was given a dangerous assignment. The pay was very good.'

'You may be right,' Peter's nose twitched. 'Why do I stand here talking to you? You're . . . you're carrion.' He started to turn away, then thought better of it. 'Do you have any idea what I am paid?'

Ryder thought for a moment. If the Russian Colonel Schroeder ran things as his American counterpart did, the pay was low but the expense account was unlimited. It had something to do with bookkeeping and budgets, Ryder recalled. The salary budget had to look low in case of unlikely Congressional scrutiny, but the expense budget could be sloughed off and lost in some larger agency, perhaps the CIA. Then, too, the Colonel's people never spent their salaries. Having no fixed residence, they had no rent to pay, no families to maintain. The money, tax-free, was simply deposited in a convenient bank and each person lived his cover identity of the moment on expense account funds. Ryder found it hard to remember what his annual salary was at the moment because one of the Colonel's girls simply forged Ryder's endorsement each month and deposited the paycheck to his account in an Arlington bank. The last figure he could remember was eight-thousand a year. Standards of living and comparative salaries being what they were, Peter was probably making around four or five thousand.

'Twenty thousand?' Ryder hazarded.

Peter looked disgusted. 'You Americans have no conception of the world around you,' he said. 'I am paid, in your money, four thousand a year. Do you know that there are boys graduating high school in this country today who will earn more than that on their first job?'

'How can you live on it?' Ryder asked innocently. 'Oh, I forgot your Waldorf salary.'

'Immaterial,' Peter brandished the knife handle at Ryder. 'You have probably been paid more for this one job than I get in a year.'

'You see,' Ryder countered gleefully, 'still another reason why you wouldn't hire me for the long haul. You're too cheap.'

'In a few hours you will be paid a sum that . . .'

'Oh, of course,' Ryder cut in. 'To save that man's life, fifty-thousand is a bargain. But now that I have a line on your regular pay scale, I think I could make more money organizing your boys. You need a good union.'

Unwillingly, Peter smiled. He returned to the couch and sat down again. 'You are very atypical but very American,' he said then. 'You are one of these international adventurers whose talents for shady operation are in constant demand. You have been associating with the scum of the earth, my friend, but you have managed to preserve your sense of humor.'

'You wouldn't want me to cry over it, would you?'

'I . . .' Peter hesitated. 'I don't know,' he said. 'I imagine humor is your way of remaining sane. And yet . . .' He seemed unable to continue.

'And yet,' Ryder prompted, 'you really do want me to cry, don't you?'

Peter's hands moved aimlessly, as if to help mold his thoughts. The blade of the steak knife glinted in Ryder's eyes.

'Perhaps so,' Peter said finally. 'It may be a romantic streak in me. I seem unconsciously to expect evil people to feel remorse.'

'You know, of course, that there isn't an American in the land who wouldn't call you an evil person.'

'Probably,' Peter laughed again. 'Probably.'

'And yet you don't cry,' Ryder persisted. 'You laugh.'

Peter nodded, his face going dead again. 'What else is there to do? There simply aren't enough tears in the whole world.'

'Ah, I call that a profoundly Russian thought.'

Peter shrugged and reached for Ryder's cigarettes. 'If you will,' he said. 'I was born in the Ukraine, in Kievgubernya, but you can call it a Russian thought if you wish. More verbal shorthand.' He lighted a cigarette. 'Perhaps we all use shorthand because we don't wish to spell things out too clearly. We might not like what we would then see.'

'Not only Russian,' Ryder said, 'but, of course, a philosopher.'

Peter blew a long plume of smoke into the air between them. 'I cannot agree,' he

160

said slowly. 'A philosopher is a man with inner beliefs who . . .' He stopped himself and inhaled on the cigarette again. 'What time is it?'

'Five-thirty. You know,' Ryder continued quickly, 'I told you what I believed in, but you've avoided telling me your side of it.'

Peter frowned at his cigarette ash and turned it slowly, examining it with great care. 'I may have done so,' he said, deepening his scrutiny, 'but not knowingly.'

'Then you do believe in something?'

'Umm.' Peter concluded his examination almost unwillingly. 'Did you perhaps at one time serve with Billy Graham, my friend? Are you trying to convert me?'

'I just think you owe me a response to my own confession.'

'That may be. Well, then . . .' Peter started to inspect the cigarette again and, realizing what he was doing, stopped it. 'You may say that I believe in myself, as do you. But I also believe in my job and in doing it successfully. Yes, there it is.'

'Nothing more?'

Peter's glance swept past Ryder, avoiding his eyes. 'Must there be more?'

'What happened to Marx and Lenin?'

'There is no reason for you to . . .'

'And the dictatorship of the proletariat?' Ryder cut in more strongly. 'And the world revolution? None of that?'

'You have no ri—.'

'And the heroes of the *Potemkin*? Of Stalingrad? They died for nothing?'

'Look here, you . . .'

'But I forgot,' Ryder taunted him, 'you're not a philosopher. He's a man with inner beliefs.'

Peter jumped to his feet and stood over Ryder, his face dark with blood, the blotch under his eye an angry purple-black. 'In your mouth, my friend, this all has a strange sound.' He was breathing heavily and trying to control the level of his voice, but it kept going higher. 'You have heroes, too, my friend. You have your Bunker Hills and Bataans and Belleau Woods. You have your bastion of democracy, too, your people's capitalism, your mission to keep the world free. But you, my super-patriotic friend, my sold-out friend, my Judas, your motives are none of these, are they?' He brought his voice back to a low, hurt murmur by an almost visible act of will. 'Are they?' he persisted.

Thinking of his Henderson personality, Ryder realized that he could no longer argue along this line with Peter. But if he were only able to tell him what he really was, Ryder promised himself, if he could only reveal his true identity, then everything would be . . . would be . . .

'Your motives are none of these,' Peter said. 'Are they?'

Ryder moistened his lips, and reached for the cigarette pack. It was empty. He said nothing for a long moment, feeling the empty cellophane and foil, feeling the nothingness inside the pack.

'Do you . . . ?' Ryder's voice croaked out and he cleared his throat. 'Do you by any chance,' he went on in a low, flat voice, 'have any cigarettes?'

CHAPTER SEVENTEEN

Ryder dozed. He hadn't meant to and the sleep itself lasted only a matter of a few minutes. It happened strangely, for him.

At first, thinking about the forbidden questions of his own motives and Peter's, he had closed his eyes as a way of hiding his

163

thoughts from the other man. As his mind moved into this unfamiliar territory his thinking looped out wider until he knew that his thoughts were not quite rational. Sleep came soon after.

After less than five minutes Ryder awoke. It had been time enough, he noted, for Peter to relax his vigil. The man leaned forward in his chair eyes closed, mouth open.

Ryder felt a faint twinge of sympathy for him. The poor devil had taken quite a bit of physical punishment in the past few hours. With his 'prisoner' asleep, Peter had allowed himself the luxury of a small nap.

Ryder shifted position on the bed, but maintained the even, slow rhythm of his breathing. A professional like Peter, with a professional's never-quite-asleep alertness, could be awakened by even a subconscious hint of danger.

Ryder could remember a time in Australia, in the back room of a seedy dockside bar in Melbourne, when he had been close to falling-down drunk, having matched his prowess at drinking whisky with the hefty second mate of a small Panamanian freighter. The mate had won—almost.

As he lay on the gritty floor in the half dark, Ryder's subconscious registered the thin, businesslike snick of a well-oiled spring knife. He had been able to gather his feet under him in time to launch a wild, flying double kick at the mate's head as the knife plunged toward him.

That had been so long ago, nineteen-forty-what? Seven? Eight? The freighter was loading canned beef and dried staples for a trading ship through the islands of Southeast Asia. The second mate had been loading a cargo of his own: counterfeit five-pound notes and Dutch guilders, antipersonnel grenades, a small high-speed multilith press, a supply of ink and paper.

Except for the grenades and the bogus it all would have been innocent enough. But the total combination was a well considered do-it-yourself kit for revolutionaries. It was the fortieth such kit the apparatus had carried into Southeast Asia that year. The guns came by another route, south and west from Hong Kong and Macao. They were the problem of another of Colonel Schroeder's operatives. But the multilith presses were of the finest quality, American-made; they came the long way from New Orleans via the Canal. And they were Ryder's problem.

His original orders were to replace the second mate and somehow muddle through the voyage, hoping to make contact along the way with others in the opposition's apparatus. The plan was one of Schroeder's rare duds. After the fight in the bar Ryder saw how idiotic it had been to think he could successfully replace the second mate.

Instead he improvised. Ryder got aboard the freighter while the mate lay sleeping on the floor of the bar, tied up with a length of electric wire. Ryder got into the hold and finally found the carton in which a gross of one-pint cans of offset-printing ink were stored. Into each can he introduced less than a c.c. of oil-based staphylococcus culture. As the quick-breaking Pacific dawn brightened the deserted dock, Ryder left the ship and waited under cover until well after seven when the mate, nursing a terrible head, stumbled aboard the freighter.

A coded cable to Singapore set the rest of the plan in motion. In the lands to which the freighter would go staphylococcus was something of an exotic rarity. Instances of the infection were ridiculously easy to spot.

Schroeder, of course, had been terribly

upset by this turn of events. Ryder could still remember the lecture he had gotten afterwards. Schroeder had been especially angry because a charge of germ warfare, while it could not be proved, could in a vague way be made to stick. After all, American printing ink had caused the disease. Nevertheless, Ryder reflected now, the final score had drawn no complaints. In all, two hundred people in the apparatus, scattered over five countries of Southeast Asia, had been identified and reported as undesirable aliens.

It had taken the apparatus nearly a year to replace them.

In the quiet of the Waldorf bedroom now, Ryder watched as Peter slept. Ryder wondered if perhaps Peter had served his apprenticeship in Southeast Asia. Despite the setback Ryder had handled it, the apparatus had gone on to significant triumphs. Of the five small countries in which Operation Staphylococcus had been conducted, two now openly leaned toward the Soviet bloc while the others remained on the fence, taking bribes from both sides. In the end, Ryder thought, it had come to nothing.

Q—By 'nothing' are we to assume you

regret this whole futile episode?

A—It was a job. I was given it. I did it. And . . .

Q—And?

A—And like so many of my jobs—and so many of Peter's—it eventually came to nothing.

Ryder gave up watching Peter and closed his eyes again. For every thrust, a parry. For every parry, a counter-thrust. He tried to doze.

It had been wrong of him to tease Peter about his political beliefs. No one in this business could afford the luxury of beliefs. You were there in the front lines. They told you to do this. You did it. Do that. Do something else. No point in thinking about it because thinking had the fatal ability to make you ask questions.

Ryder could remember another time he had gotten into one of these silly ideological-political hassles. It had been on a rare occasion when Schroeder had used two people in tandem, making them known to each other beforehand. It was Ryder's extreme ill-fortune to be paired with an absolutely green operative, a girl hardly five years out of Radcliffe who had apparently been recruited through her

168

fiancé, posthumously, so to speak. Ryder had met the man once or twice before the idiot had somehow fallen off the aft deck of the dusk ferry from Calais to Dover and been chopped into chunks by screws.

Like her fiancé, the girl was careless and ideology-ridden; a lean, small-breasted girl of about five-eight with a short torso and long, supple legs. When she curled up in a chair—as no girl that tall was ever well-advised to do—she resolved into a tangle of ankle, knee, and thigh somewhat like an unkempt pile of well-sanded lumber. She had a French sort of name: Martine or Nicole or ... Michele. Yes. Born in Des Moines and christened Michele.

Each had booked a bedroom on the Paris-Trieste train, adjoining rooms. Schroeder and Kittredge had briefed Ryder and told Michele to pick up her orders from him. Her fiancé had been dead less than a year and she herself had been in the organization no more than eight months. This assignment, her first, was easy enough if she simply took orders.

At that particular period, Ryder recalled, Tito had abruptly moved as far out of the Soviet orbit as possible, watching to see what happened in the aftermath of Stalin's death. The crackdown on Stalinists in the Yugoslav party had been fierce enough to convince even Schroeder.

At the same time, through a channel the British had somehow opened up, one of the German rocket scientists taken by the Russians near Peenemünde had allowed himself to be smuggled out of Dneipropetrovsk on a through freight to Belgrade. In his head, Schroeder had been given to believe, the scientist held absolutely up-to-the-second information on current Soviet missile work.

The first night on the train Ryder unfolded as much of the plan as he felt Michele needed to know: They were a young married couple: they would rent a Fiat in Trieste, complete with sleeping bag and other camping paraphernalia; they would take a leisurely trip down through Yugoslavia, giving themselves four days to rendezvous with the British group who would, by then, have brought the German out of Belgrade and into a rural hiding place in the mountains off the Adriatic coast.

The Fiat had an Abarth conversion job, impossible to spot except by the twin exhaust pipes. Certain other things had been done, reboring, supercharging, and the rest. The engine was capable of pushing the little car at an effortless ninety an hour. Once they picked up the German, Ryder and Michele were to streak back to Trieste and over the Italian border to where an Air Force jet would be waiting. Seven hours later, all three would be in Virginia, talking to Schroeder.

On the second night aboard the train, after they had pulled out of Vienna, Michele finished a half-litre of Reisling in the dining car during their evening meal. Back in her bedroom she opened a fifth of Ballantine's she had brought with her, it seemed, all the way from the States. Since Michele did most of the drinking she soon launched herself on a long and depressingly unoriginal monologue about her fiancé, whom she had met while he was at Harvard and she at Radcliffe, and of their burning mission in life.

'I mean one ought to understand,' she said for perhaps the fifth time since dinner, 'what one is and stands for. Jack always did. I admire a man who does. And now, I mean, in a sense, I'm doing a man's job, carrying on where he ... I mean one's not giving oneself airs or anything when one says a thing like that, is one?'

'One is,' Ryder said in a flat, unsympathetic voice. He was worried, not so much by the drinking, but by the fact that she seemed so practiced at it.

'I mean you must understand that I understood none of this,' Michele went on, 'when I first met Jack. He told me none of it. I mean, I was a real virgin.'

Ryder stood up. 'Good night, Michele.'

'Not really a virgin in the purest sense,' she amended. 'I mean, at finishing school the games mistress initiated me into the Lesbian mystery. One must experience so much in a life that one's almost glad to have certain experiences over and done with early in that life.'

Ryder opened the door to the aisle. 'Good night.'

'But, I mean, Jack was a very masculine man,' she continued. 'Very much the virile man, like you.'

Ryder's eyes narrowed. 'Go to sleep, you sot.'

Michele stood up, weaving slightly, and shoved the door shut. 'I mean you can kiss me now.'

'Stand away from the door.'

'Or anything else you want to.

Absolutely anything.'

Ryder grabbed her by the shoulders and shook her steadily forward and back. 'Now, listen,' he began, shaking her in the same emphatic tempo of his words. 'I don't care why you're in this. Loyalty, ideology, kicks. Whatever brought you here, you'll behave. You foul us up and you'll abort the whole mission. So calm down, you flat-chested bitch, and go to sleep and stay off the sauce till this is over and done with. Do you read me?'

She nodded. 'Loud and clear.' Her hand darted down his belly. 'And after tonight, I solemnly promise I'll . . .'

The entire job turned into Operation Scatterbrain. It was only the simplicity of the job and the relative absence of any real danger that kept them out of Sovint hands. The girl was as undisciplined as an alley-cat and totally unable to take orders. The only control Ryder had over her was to ration what sexual relations they enjoyed. As a method of control it had its good points and its bad. Once he understood how to use it, it worked.

After the jet landed them at Friendship Airport near Baltimore, Ryder and the girl parted company. He brought the German to Schroeder. The fugitive unburdened himself of enough information on Russian rocketry to fill 3600 feet of recording tape. The gist of his report was that the Russians had booster troubles, primarily in the fuel feed valves and mixers. The day after this comforting mass of information had been transcribed, typed, mimeographed and distributed to the CIA and other agencies, the Russians orbited their first satellite.

Ryder was in New York the next morning at the apartment Michele kept in Greenwich Village off Sheridan Square. He was lying face down on a couch, re-reading a tabloid headline:

RED BABY MOON
ORBITING EARTH

'Red baby moon,' he hummed, 'shine down on me.'

'Hm?' Michele came in from the kitchen carrying two tumblers half full of Ballantine's. 'Welcome to New York.'

Ryder rolled on his side to look up at her. Without clothes she was much more attractive. The loose dresses she wore to conceal the smallness of her breasts only served to emphasize the situation. Bare, her breasts were still small but at least had form, cast shadows, and proclaimed their actual existence. Without the unfitted dress, too, her waistline was narrower, stressing the fact that she did, indeed, have hips.

Ryder took the tumbler of Scotch and sat up on the couch, swinging his feet to the floor. He lifted his drink and stared for a moment at the two tiny ice cubes in it.

'*Ave atque vale*,' he said, by way of a toast.

'Nasty thought,' she said, touching her glass to his. 'Why "hail and farewell"? I mean you're here for the weekend at least, aren't you?' She sat down beside him and relaxed against the end arm of the couch, spreading her legs over his lap.

'No, I'm not.' Ryder sipped his drink.

Her toes wiggled. 'But, I mean, I thought you were on leave. I am.'

'No, you're not.'

She began to trace a line over his ear by stroking his hair with a big toe. 'But I am,' she insisted.

'Take a drink,' Ryder suggested. He watched her reduce the contents of her glass by a third. 'I'm on duty,' he said then. 'My duty is to tell you that you aren't on leave. You're discharged. You no longer work for us.'

Slowly, Michele put the glass on the floor beside her. By a kind of reflex, her legs slid off Ryder's lap. The skin across her belly looked suddenly tight. 'But why?'

'Schroeder can't afford anybody as fancy as you.'

'You bastard,' she said softly.

'Oh?'

'You told him, didn't you.'

'Of course I told him.'

'But it was a personal thing between the two of us.'

'Wrong.'

She jumped to her feet and began to pace angrily from the couch to the door. Ryder watched the way her rump muscles twitched impatiently as she turned. 'I mean I assumed you were some rudimentary kind of gentleman who . . . But you actually told everything that we . . . ? I mean, everything?'

Ryder stood up, took his jacket from the chair where he had dropped it and shoved his arm through one sleeve. 'I'm due back tonight,' he said. 'This red baby moon means the Kraut was a phony plant or something. It's easy to see now how we

176

latched onto him with so little trouble.' He finished putting on his jacket and walked to the door, pushing her gently out of the way as he passed. Her skin felt cold.

'Goddamn you!' she burst out. 'What am I supposed to do now?'

Ryder considered for a moment. 'Get a job here in New York. Write off the whole thing as a ... a lark. Go into something ... oh, maybe Communications. Advertising? The agencies are full of kooks. Find a job that's tuned to your wavelength, Michele. There are plenty of them.'

'You utter bastard,' she said. Her breath had become unsteady. 'I thought you understood what this job meant to me.'

'Not at first,' Ryder admitted. 'But you finally made things clear.'

'I mean about Jack and me,' she said, shaking her head angrily. Her eyes were moist now. 'About carrying on his work. You haven't the slightest understanding of how important all of this is to our way of life, have you? To our country's posture in the world? No, not you. You're just a paid employee, a mercenary, a ... a ...'

'A hired gun.' He grinned wryly. 'Good-by, Michele.'

'To-to you it's j-just a job, isn't it?' She was starting to cry.

Ryder nodded. 'That's the only way to think of it, a job and do the best way you can. I wanted to dump you after that night on the train. But the British team was expecting a man and a woman. The trip from Trieste would've looked awfully peculiar for one man by himself. If I hadn't needed you, I'd have gotten rid of you long before we hit Trieste. You're unreliable, Michele. You haven't the vaguest idea of what discipline means. All you have is a very high-flown, half-baked ideology and a terrible twitch in the loins. It isn't enough.'

'And you?' she sobbed. 'What's your ideology?'

'Not like yours.'

'I t-tremble for us,' she said, 'if we have to depend on unthinking, unfeeling oafs like you, hirelings, bought and paid-for hirelings.'

'And if we depended on people like you?' Ryder snapped. 'Amateurs?' he added in a curdling tone. 'Rank, stinking amateurs who think this is some new kind of charades or guessing game or treasure hunt?'

'Yes? We'd be far better . . .'

'We'd be dead, darling,' Ryder cut in. 'Tito's cops would've had us deported in twenty-four hours. Or else Sovint would've left us under a pile of stones.'

She sniffed. 'And your precious German,' she pounced, 'would never have come here to tell us all those lies.'

Ryder laughed suddenly, a sound that was unpleasant to his ears. 'You're comic, Michele. Good-by.' He turned the doorknob.

'I'll tell everything I know about Colonel Schroeder,' she warned him. 'I'll tell about Jack and how they let him get killed and about you and the German and everything.'

'To whom?' Ryder asked. 'What newspaper would print it?' He opened the door to the hall outside. 'You've got your accumulated pay and a month's severance besides. You've enough to live on till you find a job. Just try to calm down and forget about the whole thing.'

She rubbed her cheek to dry it. 'Just like that?'

'There's no other way to do it, Michele. Good-by.'

'When . . .?' She paused for a moment, looking at him. 'When do you have to get back?'

'Tonight.'

'But it's still morning.'

'So?'

She swung the door wide. 'I mean, you can't just leave without one for the road. My Lord, there are so many things we didn't have time to try.'

On his bed in the room at the Waldorf, Ryder shifted suddenly with the memory. The small noise he made awakened Peter. 'Yes?' he asked.

'Nothing,' Ryder assured him. 'Absolutely nothing.'

The two men settled down again to wait.

CHAPTER EIGHTEEN

The church bells rang nine times. Since five-thirty neither Ryder nor Peter had spoken except to exchange information about the time. From Park Avenue far below, the sound of heavy traffic, auto horns, the squeal of brakes, filtered up to them in a muted whisper.

At about now, Ryder decided, the big Tupolev 104 jet was crossing the arctic wastes north of the British Isles on a great circle route that would bring it over Newfoundland and New England to Idlewild, where the traffic pattern would have been cleared for it to land immediately. The reception party, now, was just beginning to take shape. The Mayor and our UN delegate were checking their schedule for the day, thinking of the arrival at Idlewild later and the motorcade back to the Waldorf. At this moment, Connell was entering Klein's down on Union Square to buy a sturdy, one-piece, forest green coverall. He would take it to the 14th Street flophouse-hotel room he had rented this morning, get the coverall wet, smear it with dirt and grease, crumple and wring it, then let it dry. Everyone was busy, Ryder thought, but they would all pause for a fateful ten seconds this afternoon when the motorcade stopped outside the Waldorf. There would be a slight pause then. The pause heard 'round the world.

Lying on the living room couch, dressed in his shirt and trousers, but too tired to bend over and lace his shoes, Ryder tried to evaluate Connell's thinking in the event that he tried to get into this room at the crucial moment and found the door permanently barred. Or, found it open and, entering, walked into Peter's knife.

If Peter were as intelligent as he seemed, he would leave the door unlocked. The man had probably thought it out that far in advance; he knew that if Connell could not get into the room he would find some other vantage point for his afternoon's work. So the door would be open. Peter would assume that Connell would be armed. Knife against gun? All Peter could do would be to delay Connell a few seconds. But wouldn't that be long enough to abort his mission? The thing was timed to mere seconds. Even a short delay might undo it.

Ryder realized that his best course of action was the simplest. He would wait until Peter opened the door for Connell, let Connell shoot Peter—or cow him with the gun, a remote possibility—and then helpfully relieve Connell of the gun so that he could be free to drop the grenades. Once he held the gun, Ryder decided, the whole game was over. Connell would be stopped, Peter would be kept silent, K would go unharmed and Sovint would not get a would-be assassin for the propaganda people to advertise.

Colonel Schroeder couldn't have

foreseen all the kinks in the basic plan but he would probably mark the revisions acceptable.

Ryder sighed and closed his eyes. K was soaring high over the arctic. The Mayor was attending to his morning business. Connell was buying coveralls. Everyone was busy but him. He opened his eyes and turned to watch Peter, sitting on a chair he had tilted back against the front door. He was turning his knife over and over again, first this way, then that, in an effort to keep himself awake without hypnotizing himself.

'Nine o'clock, Peter,' Ryder announced in a loud voice.

Peter looked up, startled, then glanced at his wristwatch and nodded. He got up and went to the phone on the living room desk. 'Pick it up,' he ordered. Ryder sighed again and stood up. Padding across the room on stockinged feet, he lifted the phone. 'May I help you?' the operator asked. 'Outside line, please,' Ryder said.

Peter took the phone from him and turned it so that the dial was hidden. He motioned Ryder away from him with an outthrust palm, then shifted the knife to his left hand and dialled a number quickly.

Ryder watched him, wondering how easily Peter could be disarmed if the need ever arose. He decided that it would be an interesting and possibly painful experiment, but that it could be done. They waited.

'Fifty,' Peter said suddenly. 'Now. And my cousins aren't to know.' He listened for a moment, then hung up.

Interesting, Ryder thought. The bagman was to get here without being seen by the Sovint people. Evidently Peter's run-in last night had convinced him that his 'cousins' had to be left out of it. But why, Ryder asked himself. He wondered, abruptly, whether Peter himself knew the answer. It didn't seem likely.

Stepping away from the phone, Peter gestured toward it. 'Have them send up some breakfast,' he said then. 'If they make it fast, we can be finished by the time the money arrives.'

Ryder picked up the phone. 'Scrambled eggs and ham?'

Peter shrugged. 'Anything that can be brought up quickly.'

Ryder listened for the operator. When she failed to come on, he jiggled the receiver cradle up and down several times.

He waited, jiggling it more slowly now to make the switchboard light flash on and off regularly. 'Something's wrong,' he said at last. 'I'm not getting side tone.'

Peter's eyes widened very slightly. 'Step away from the phone,' he ordered. Then, picking it up, he listened for a moment, frowning. He blew softly into the microphone, then more loudly. Finally, he whistled into it. 'You are right,' he said. 'The line has been disconnected.'

'Even so,' Ryder said, 'the operator can pull the cord but you'll still get side tone if you . . .'

'I know,' Peter cut in brusquely. 'Do you take me for a fool? The line is dead somewhere between here and the switchboard.'

They stood there watching each other for a long moment. Then Peter jerked his thumb at the couch. 'Sit down and stay down,' he commanded. When Ryder had done so, Peter unscrewed the mouthpiece cap and picked out the microphone. He studied the wires leading from it, then replaced it and unscrewed the receiver end. 'Amazing,' he said then, putting the telephone back together again. He replaced the phone on its cradle and opened a drawer of the desk. Placing the phone inside it, he looked quickly about him.

'I'll get some,' Ryder said, standing up. 'I'll be good don't worry.'

He went into the bedroom and returned almost at once with both pillows from the bed. Handing them to Peter, he lay down on the couch again.

Peter folded the pillows around the phone and closed the drawer, hiding the whole business. Then, shutting the door to the bedroom where the other phone was located, he moved swiftly to the front door and removed the chair propped against it. Gently taking the doorknob in his hands, he turned it slowly and pulled. The door failed to move. Turning the knob the other way, he pulled again without budging the door. Ryder felt his own heart pause for a long beat.

Peter stood back, stared at the door for a moment, then whirled on Ryder. 'Amazing,' he repeated in a flat tone of near disgust. 'One would never credit them with such thoroughness. Every telephone on how many floors? Two, three? It must have taken days.'

'You don't know how sensitive the bedroom microphone is,' Ryder pointed out. 'It may be able to pick up right through the door.'

'It cannot be helped.' Peter turned back to stare at the unmoving front door. 'They must have actuated the double-lock.'

'The key acts as a bolt on this side of the door,' Ryder explained. 'One turn releases the regular lock. A second turn releases the double-lock.' He reached in his pocket. 'Here,' he said, throwing Peter the key. He watched him ease it carefully into the lock and turn it unsuccessfully to either side. 'Won't move?'

'Not even half a turn.'

'Clever,' Ryder said. 'That takes care of the moneyman, doesn't it?'

Peter stared at the floor between his feet. 'I wonder,' he mused.

'What do you wonder?' Ryder asked. 'Why we've been locked in?'

'That, yes.'

'You aren't in any doubt as to who did it?'

'None.'

'Just why they did do it.'

'Yes,' Peter admitted.

Ryder paused, putting his thoughts in order. The thing was almost unbelievable but a mind like Peter's should reach the inescapable conclusion within the next few seconds. Nevertheless, it had to be said.

'There can be only one reason,' Ryder said in a slow voice.

'Yes?' Peter looked up, his eyes clouded with thought.

'They want you to fail.'

Peter's eyes widened. In that instant Ryder realized that he had over-estimated Peter. The man was intelligent, but he had blind spots like anyone else. And the thing Ryder had suddenly realized, the monstrous thing he now suggested, remained invisible to Peter because it was too incredible to be believed.

'I ... I don't understand ... you.' Peter's voice sounded draggy, as though he were fighting off the effects of a drug.

'They don't want you to stop the assassination, Peter.' Ryder stood up and stared into the eyes of his opposite number. 'They want K to die.'

The two men watched each other's eyes with an odd intensity. Peter's mouth twitched, paused, moved again.

'You,' he whispered. '*Who are you?*'

CHAPTER NINETEEN

There were no other rules for this sort of situation, Ryder reflected, except the cardinal rule that one never broke cover identity. In another operation to which the Colonel might assign two of his people without letting either know that he had a friend on hand, the entire project might grind to a conclusion before either friend suspected. In this instance, however, the cardinal rule was not only quite clear but, in the circumstances, more stringently applicable than ever. One simply didn't break cover to one's opposite number. Ryder could not imagine a situation that the Colonel would agree justified such a breach of security and yet...

He sighed and looked away from Peter. And yet, he told himself, if ever there were such a moment, it was now.

'I'm a cop,' Ryder said then, deciding on a half-truth policy. 'I'm not from Chicago nor am I Henderson. I'm Sergeant John Ryder, Special Department, New York City Police.' He took a long slow breath, concealing the movement to avoid a tell-tale sign of lying.

Peter watched him rather closely for a moment, the knife held ready for instant action. Then he smiled coldly. 'Ridiculous,' he snapped. 'At a time like this, you choose to tell me fairy tales.'

Ryder turned his hands palms up in an international gesture of openness. 'I can't help how it sounds, Peter. It's the truth and we're both stuck with it.'

'Sheer nonsense,' Peter retorted, the knife still slanted toward Ryder. 'Whatever you are you must understand that the situation is desperate. In order to succeed, we must be frank with each other. Do you understand?'

Ryder nodded, understanding him all too well. 'It was over a year ago. The Commissioner felt certain the conference would be held here. He wanted every assurance that there would be no assassination attempt in his city. Four of us were assigned to the Sons, four of us to the Memphis group and two to the west coast organization. A year later, here I am. My one purpose in being here is to see that no attempt is made. There simply isn't any more to tell.'

Peter's head had started to shake from

side to side in the middle of Ryder's speech. Now it continued to shake but more slowly and emphatically. 'I cannot accept this story,' he said then. 'There are just too many holes in it, my friend.'

'Go ahead. Everything has a logical explanation.'

'Which you will proceed to invent,' Peter added, smiling coldly again. 'Very well. Let us begin with the most gaping hole of all. Why did you find it necessary to protect K, as you call him, by the complicated and dangerous method of joining his would-be assassins? Is this how you protect your President from possible attack? No. Is this how you protect other visiting dignitaries? I doubt it. Then why in this one case? And why by such a devious method?'

'That's the simplest answer of all.'

'Proceed.'

'If you know anything about guarding a public figure, and I'm quite sure you do, you understand that the only foolproof way is to stand beside him at all times, to ring him with a curtain of alert human flesh. Granted?'

'Yes, of course,' Peter said impatiently. 'Go on.'

'We assumed that K would be

surrounded by his own people who would remain as alert as was humanly possible. But it's one thing for our Secret Service to protect our President in our own cities, where every twist of the road, every profile of the buildings, every possible alleyway and niche is known and can be anticipated. It becomes even easier because the Secret Service can depend on complete cooperation from local police. When they need that cooperation they ask for it and get it.'

'This is your simple answer?' Peter asked.

'It's not finished. We knew that your people couldn't possibly know New York City the way we do. We also knew that they would probably not ask for help. Even if they did, they would suspect that help and refuse to trust it. In any event, they did not ask for help.'

'That much,' Peter admitted, 'is true.'

'All this was foreseen a year ago,' Ryder continued. 'The Russian character may be confusing at times, but its suspiciousness is always predictable.'

'Its suspiciousness of American help, yes.'

'All right,' Ryder went on. 'Since we

192

couldn't get right next to K, we knew we couldn't do a foolproof job of guarding him. We also knew that any job we tried would be an outside job, yards away from him, with suspicious Russian cops between us and him. We considered that, under the circumstances, he had an excellent chance of being knocked off.'

'Why didn't that please you?' Peter wanted to know.

'Why, you bonehead? Because we love him, do you think?'

Peter's mouth split into a real grin. 'My God!' he said. 'It's the American philosophy of public relations. I see it all. It would be bad public relations if he were murdered here in your greatest city while on a mission of peace.' He chuckled for a moment. 'How could anyone have foreseen this?' he asked himself aloud. 'The British tradition in America. Fair play, hospitality, the handshake, the formal smile, even to hated enemies.' He sat down on the edge of the couch and stared at the floor, still laughing quietly to himself. The knife, Ryder noted, was still held in readiness.

'Something more than that,' Ryder said. 'I don't expect you to believe it, but we all wanted this conference to mean something.

We wanted it to get somewhere. We didn't want tragedy before it even started.'

Peter's lower lip stuck out and he shrugged. 'Possible,' he commented. 'Possible, that is, that you yourself feel that way. Impossible that it should be the official policy of the New York City Police Department.' He seemed to consider this for a moment. 'In any event,' he said, 'go on.'

'What more can I tell you?'

'Umm. Tell me . . . yes, tell me how long the Police Department has been recruiting and training men of your advanced calibre?' Peter glanced up mockingly. 'Tell me that, Sergeant Ryder.'

'Do you find it hard to believe?'

'Hard, no.' Peter stood up and laughed once. 'Impossible, yes.' He pitched the knife onto the desk.

Ryder watched the knife clatter on the desk top and lie there, equally distant from both men. 'Then why have you disarmed yourself?' he asked.

Peter walked to the window and spread the curtains aside. 'I think we can drop the whole discussion, my friend,' he said after a moment, his back to Ryder as he peered out the window. 'We understand each other.'

Ryder lay down on the couch and closed his eyes. 'Connell,' he began in a tired monotone, 'is disguised as an electrician. He enters the building shortly before K arrives. I report some burnt-out bulbs. Connell arrives at my room carrying light bulbs a minute or two before K reaches the front entrance. The rest you can imagine.'

'Grenades?'

'Two of them.'

'Mills?'

Ryder nodded, then realized that Peter could not see the movement. 'Yes,' he said. 'But Connell will find the door locked. He'll have to improvise.'

'Good. He will waste so much time finding another room that he'll be too late.'

'Possibly so,' Ryder admitted. 'But he's a very flexible man. If he misses his chance, he'll find another.'

'Not much chance of that.'

'Agreed,' Ryder said. 'But if there's a chance, Connell will find it and take it. He's not to be underestimated.'

'I see. In other words, we must find a way to make sure the door is open and Connell can walk right into our arms.'

'In other words, yes.'

Ryder heard the other man walk past him to the door. He opened his eyes and watched Peter stare at the lock. 'We have very little chance of that,' Peter said finally. 'This is beginning to get uncomfortably close.'

'Can you get any help from your S—' Ryder paused a split second, not wanting to use the professional slang word 'Sovint,' and turned the sibilance into 'sidekicks.' 'Is there one or two of them who can help you out?'

Peter turned to face him. 'Ponamarenko is evidently carrying instructions none of the rest know about.'

'Bullneck?'

Peter nodded. 'And since he is in charge of the entire detail, his orders will be obeyed, no matter how odd they seem.'

'So we can't count on any of his subordinates? Not even if you were to tell them what Ponamarenko has in mind?'

'You have a good ear for difficult names, my friend,' Peter said. 'A trained ear. The New York City Police do a thorough job on their men.' He smiled for a second and then his face went dead again. 'No,' he went on, 'none of them know me. Not one of them would believe me. And if one did, he would still not countermand Ponamarenko's orders.'

Ryder watched him for a long moment. 'You have a very adaptable mind, Peter,' he said at last. 'A few minutes ago you were shocked to realize what they were trying to do. Now it doesn't seem to bother you much at all.'

'Bother? No, not that. Such things are not unheard of, you understand. And, of course, the moment you told me, I could see the logical beauty of it. Two birds with one stone. He would be removed and your country would be blamed. The faction that planned this is playing for very high stakes, indeed.'

'Any idea who they are?'

'Would that interest the New York City Police?'

When Ryder failed to answer, Peter leaned with his back against the locked door and looked grimly at nothing for a moment. 'You can be assured, my friend, that when we get out of this, the faction that Ponamarenko represents will be liquidated long before your, ah, Police Department can make any use of them.'

Ryder poked out his lower lip and shrugged, in a perfect parody of Peter.

'Immaterial,' he said. 'But I was happy to hear you say "when we get out." I would take a somewhat dimmer view.'

Neither man spoke for a moment. Ryder glanced at his watch. Nine-fifteen. Connell had bought the coveralls and was leaving Klein's. Still plenty of time, long, aching hours of it, enough time for two bright people to think their way out of this.

The windows of the suite, he knew, had a slight ledge that a really desperate man might make use of in getting to an adjoining suite. But the suites on either side were most probably occupied by Bullneck's people. Trying the tied-sheet routine in an effort to get to a lower floor by the outside of the building was equally fruitless. You might end up in Sovint territory or you might be spotted from the street and arrested by the cops. In either case, Connell would still remain at large.

The door would certainly yield to some kind of manipulation. It might be picked clear of whatever they had done to jam it. The hinges might be removed. As a last resort, it could be broken open. But the hall outside was certainly under Sovint surveillance. Ryder shifted uncomfortably on the couch. 'It's no good,' he said then.

198

'You know better than to say that,' Peter admonished him.

'I know better. But I'm entitled to get it on the record, anyway.'

'A great deal may happen in the next few hours.'

'It isn't my idea of comfort to sit here and hope something happens outside that door.'

'I almost lost sight of the fact that you are an American,' Peter said. 'We Russians have learned over the decades how to wait patiently.'

'For what? Freedom?'

Peter pushed Ryder's legs to the floor and sat down on the other end of the couch. 'Yes,' he said then, 'a good question.' He glanced at Ryder. 'And what are your Americans waiting for, my friend?'

'I wouldn't know. Personally, I'm waiting for an idea that . . .'

'Yes?'

Ryder sat up on the couch, reached for the pack of cigarettes and, finding it empty, threw the pack into a corner of the room. 'Listen closely,' he began. 'I want your most honest and realistic appraisal.'

'Go on.'

'Do you think there are any more bugs in

the suite?'

Peter frowned. 'Any more what?'

'Microphones.'

'The one we have muffled in the desk. The telephone in the bedroom, but the door is closed. Why?'

'Then what I've told you in the past few minutes couldn't have been overheard.'

'One learns never to say "couldn't," my friend.'

'Yes, but it's a chance we have to take. Now.' He turned to Peter and tapped his knees. 'How badly would it go with you if Ponamarenko got his hands on you?'

'How badly? He has his hands on me at this very moment.'

'I mean, if he didn't know anything more about me except that I was an assassin waiting to let in another assassin.'

Peter's eyes widened. 'Touché,' he said. 'First-class thinking! Good enough for export.'

CHAPTER TWENTY

Ryder turned the bathroom hot water tap on full and glanced up at Peter. They were crowded together over the sink, the door closed behind them. When the water became almost too hot to bear, Ryder placed his left forearm under it, then soaped the skin and worked up a heavy lather. Peter held the steak knife under the tap, soaped it and began washing the blade.

Wincing slightly at the heat, Ryder rinsed off the lather and inspected the pinkish skin of his arm. 'Ready?'

Peter held the soapy knife under the tap, then shook it dry in the air. 'Let's go.'

Ryder eased the bathroom door open. The two men moved silently through the bedroom to the living room, shutting the door behind them and insulating the bedroom phone from their voices. 'Now,' Peter said in a quiet undertone.

'I don't like this at all!' Ryder exclaimed. 'Where's the man with the money?' He faced the bedroom door and tried to bring his voice up from the diaphragm to project through the door as strongly as possible.

'He'll be here.'

'I'm hungry and I'm thirsty,' Ryder persisted. 'Why can't I have a drink of water?'

'Very well, then,' Peter said sulkily, opening the bedroom door rather noisily.

'Go, drink yourself sick.'

'Just tell me where the moneyman is,' Ryder went on. 'You said he'd be here by now. If you try to welsh on this, buddy, your man's as good as dead right now.'

'He'll be here.'

Ryder ran the bathroom tap as loudly as possible, shouting over the sound: 'Something wrong. I can smell it. Something's gone completely wrong.'

'Nothing is wrong,' Peter assured him, standing near the bedroom phone.

'You're acting peculiarly,' Ryder said, holding a glass under the faucet. 'First the phone went on the blink. Now you won't open the door. I think somebody's onto you. I think maybe the FBI has you taped.'

'Don't talk nonsense.'

'No?' Ryder swallowed the water noisily. 'Then where's the moneyman? Maybe the FBI nabbed him.'

'Shut up with your FBI, you fool!'

Ryder clinked the glass down on the sink. 'Watch yourself, buddy,' he snapped, moving toward Peter and the phone. 'Our deal isn't welded together, you know. Unless you pony up the money, your man's going to die. Get that through your head.'

'Keep your voice down!' Peter snapped.

'Why? You afraid the FBI's tapped the phone? Is that what you're so worried about?'

'Shut up!'

'I'll shut up the minute the money arrives.'

'It will get here.'

'Promises? You Russians are great with promises. You've been promising yourselves so much for so long, you're in the habit now.'

'I said, shut up!'

'I was a sucker to believe you, buddy. You Russians are all alike.'

'I'm warning you,' Peter said in a tight voice.

'With what, that lousy little knife! If I wanted to take that away from you, it wouldn't be hard.'

'You Americans are all great braggarts. What are you but a lot of wind?'

'Oh?' Ryder's voice got suddenly soft. 'A lot of wind?'

'Brandishing your atom bombs. A silly gesture. Look at you, my Judas friend. What a picture you make.'

'Goddamn you!' Ryder's voice took off from a low point and rose to full volume. He took a noisy step forward and grunted.

Peter stamped his foot and slapped himself hard in the stomach.

'No, you don't!' he yelped.

They grasped each other around the waist and began wrestling back and forth within a few feet of the phone, breathing heavily and cursing under their breath. Suddenly Ryder let out a sharp yelp. 'You slimy bastard!' he shouted.

Carefully, he pulled up his left shirtsleeve. Holding the edge of the knife on the still pinkish skin, Peter pursed his lips and pressed down with a short slicing motion. At first Ryder felt nothing. Then pain shot along his arm as the blood rilled up in a thin line about five inches long. He tightened his jaw until it hurt almost as much as the slash.

'You still haven't taken it away from me,' Peter said gloatingly.

'You rotten...!' Ryder's voice rose until it choked off. They grappled again, Ryder carefully smearing Peter's hand and shirt with blood, then letting some splash on the floor and bed. He stepped away from the other man and nodded. Peter stood up and closed his eyes.

Ryder pulled back his right arm and measured the distance carefully. He took a step forward with his left foot and brought his right fist up and out in a wide winging uppercut that landed just to the left of Peter's chin. 'No?' Ryder gasped. 'Haven't I, you stupid bastard?'

Peter slumped down on the floor with a satisfyingly loud thud. Ryder stood over him for a moment, gasping for breath. Then, stumbling to the door that led out of the suite, he began hammering against it as loudly as he could. 'Help!' he shouted. 'Help! Get the police! Get a doctor! Help!'

The door reverberated dully like the head of an immense bass drum. Ryder took a long breath and began pounding again. He continued for several minutes until he heard confused voices shouting to him from outside in the corridor.

CHAPTER TWENTY-ONE

'I'm terribly, terribly sorry, sir,' the house man was saying as he made his way to the front door. His glance kept straying to Ryder's bloody sleeve.

'Just see that you keep this Johnnie locked up a little better this time,' Ryder told him. 'And get that damn phone fixed.'

He and the house man turned to the doorway. Peter was dwarfed by the immense figure of Ponamarenko behind him. The big man's flat, square face showed Ryder about as much inner feeling as a slab of lard, but the meaty hand clamped on Peter's right arm told a story in itself. Ponamarenko's tiny, cupid's mouth pursed indignantly. 'A great misfortune,' he said for perhaps the fourth time in the last few minutes.

'Well, anyway,' Ryder remarked, 'I can't say my stay here's been boring.' He gave the house man a broad midwestern grin. 'You got any more like him down in Room Service?'

'Oh, good Lord, no,' the house man assured him.

Almost bowing, the three men started to leave. Ryder watched Peter's face as Ponamarenko yanked him out into the corridor. The mouth was slightly downcast, as were the eyes, all part of the crazed-waiter characterization. But as the house man closed the door, Peter looked up for an instant at Ryder, just a quick direct glance, nothing more.

Ryder sighed and glanced at his watch,

alone again in the suite. Ten A.M. of the big day, four hours until K.

Too tired to remove his shirt and trousers, he lay down on the bed and began a final evaluation. There were only three elements left in the equation: Peter, Ponamarenko, and Ryder.

Ryder closed his eyes and began sorting out Peter's itinerary during the next few hours. He would be taken back to the basement lockup, pending the arrival of the city police. The Waldorf had a lot on its mind for the next four hours. Not even the visit of Queen Elizabeth and Prince Philip had been an occasion more important than this. Peter would probably be placed in a room slightly harder to break out of than the previous one. He would nevertheless escape. A really good man could always escape from a low-security cell, if he knew he had to. He would break out and . . . what? Make contact with his own higher-up and break the news about the Russian plan to let K be murdered? Probably.

Bullneck, Ryder decided now, would understand that a basement room could not hold Peter any better this time than it had before. At large, Peter was dangerous to him. Bullneck would either help Peter escape and immobilize him far more efficiently than the Waldorf had, or wait until his escape and then do it. Then Ponamarenko would make certain that none of his own people stopped Connell during the final minutes. Once the grenades were dropped, he would descend on Ryder's suite and kill both Ryder and Connell, or hold them for the police. Unfortunately, the grenades would not drop.

Either way, Ryder saw now, Peter was going to have a rough time of it. It was inevitable that Ponamarenko would have Peter killed. Not now, of course, but later and outside the country. Just outside.

Poor Peter, Ryder thought, just an honest pro doing a good job, a better job than his higher-ups deserved. He felt a sudden anger at the old knowledge that good men always had to die because there were stupid men in the world. Exit Peter. R.I.P.

His own part of the equation, Ryder reflected, was still according to master plan. Connell would enter the suite, be slugged, drugged, trussed, and kept out of circulation until the summit conference had concluded. Keeping him out of circulation was going to be a lot harder, with Ponamarenko in the act, but once Connell's big opportunity had been blocked, subsequent events would not be as hard to handle.

There existed, nevertheless, a new danger. If he were in Bullneck's massive shoes, Ryder told himself, he'd try to nab Connell after the aborted attempt and keep him on ice to be shoved forward when Sovint itself liquidated K. Connell would be woozy with Seconal when Bullneck gave him to the police. He would hear himself being accused of killing K and he would grab at the chance to confess. Connell and Ponamarenko made a good team. The trick was to keep them apart.

Perhaps, Ryder mused, settling himself on the bed for sleep, the best thing would be to find another suite Ponamarenko wouldn't know about, head off Connell and steer him to the new location. Except, he reminded himself, that Bullneck would now be watching every move he made. It would be impossible to get free of surveillance. So much for that.

A farce, really, thought Ryder. A year of my time, sixteen months of Peter's, a lot of money from John Q. and Ivan Public,

Peter's life just to protect the life of a man slated for removal by his own palace guard anyway. No matter how you tried, it didn't really add up to one of Man's nobler efforts.

It was typical, though, of the kind of work he'd been doing for the Colonel since 1944, small jobs or big, none of them adding up to what you might call an historic contribution to civilization.

Q—Does the witness expect medals or a crying towel?

A—Neither. But this has to add up to something. Otherwise it's fifteen years of very distinguished nothing.

Q—Why should your life be more meaningful than any other man's? You've had excitement and the satisfaction of doing a job well. What more do you expect?

A—I expected something more back in 1944 when the Colonel first . . .

Q—You're snivelling like a virgin bride. Didn't Mother tell you it would be like this?

A—I'm trying to get at something important here.

Q—And if it turns out to be unimportant?

A—I'd hate even to think that.

Q—You're thinking it right now. You've been thinking it for several years. You've begun to introspect too much and ask yourself silly, virginal questions like: 'What does it all mean?' Once you get that naive, your usefulness to Colonel Schroeder is nil.

A—And the Colonel's usefulness to the country? Is he being naive? The things his people do must be done.

Q—Why?

A—Because if they're not done, we go down to defeat.

Q—That's exactly what Peter's Colonel Schroeder tells him.

Of course, Ryder told himself, twisting on the bed, aware now that he had to stop this inward-looking immediately if he wanted sleep. Of course Peter does it for the same reasons, he thought. It's a standoff. The biggest standoff in history. Now drop it and go to sleep.

He closed his eyes and immediately saw Peter, with Bullneck's fingers clamped on his arm, and that last, direct look before the door closed. The look said: 'It is now in your hands; do it well.' All right, Ryder told himself, it will be done well. Like everything else in the past fifteen years, there is no margin for error. The job is done and done well. What more can a man ask of life? Significance? Meaningful

211

accomplishment?

Let him be content in knowing that when Dr. Khereniev wanted to escape, a man provided the way. That Khereniev voluntarily returned two years later doesn't matter. Let him be content in knowing that when the Istaki government began to crumble, a man arrived with plans and money to keep it stable. Never mind that Istaki looted the treasury after six months and escaped to Switzerland. Let him feel proud of the fact that when we had to know whether Svetlov and his people had successfully mastered Process 18, a man got conclusive proof. It was not important that within a matter of weeks, both we and Svetlov discovered that Process 18 was too unstable for military application.

What difference did any of the aftermaths make? The pride had to come from the accomplishments, the jobs well done. It was fatal, Ryder assured himself, absolutely fatal to ask naive questions like 'What does it all mean?'

All right, he thought now, eyes closed, body rigid on the bed. All right, the jobs were well done. How do you feel? Satisfied? Happy? Content?

Ryder suddenly realized that he had let

himself get much too far out of hand. It was one thing to introspect; despite all the warnings, it happened now and then. It was another and much more dangerous thing to let oneself sink deeper into questions of meaning and motive until one could no longer concentrate on the job at hand.

By a deliberate effort, Ryder began relaxing all his muscles. He rolled the pillow into a tight cylinder and placed it directly under his neck. Then he made certain that the major muscles of legs and arms were loose. One by one, he eased the tension in each part of his body. One by one, he slacked off each knotted muscle until he began to experience the floating sensation of auto-hypnosis, of tremendous concentration on one's body to the exclusion of the outside and the interior worlds. At that point, fatigue took over.

He was trying to open the living room door but They had jammed it. He kicked it down and ran along the corridor, past doors, doors.

He was running past the doors, the hundreds of doors, the big and small and wide and narrow ones, all knocked together into a barricade around the demolished building. He kept trying the doors, knowing they were nailed shut, but knowing that one of them was a real door into the nothingness. They had signs on the doors, misleading ones. '500 Feet to Bar-B-Q Spareribs and Mile-Hi Malts.' He pulled at that door but it was a sham.

'Earn Big Money with a High School Diploma!' He yanked on the knob, but the door refused to budge. 'Learn Television Repair in Spare Time and Make $100 a Day!'

Ryder was pounding along the corridor, staring wild-eyed at the signs and trying the doors. He could feel his breath surging in and out of him. 'Think Big! Be Big! Buy Up to a Hard-Top, Two-Tone, Power-Steering, No-Shift Model!' His lungs started to ache. 'Mother Never Knew How Easy Washday Could Be!' A sharp pain around his heart made him gasp suddenly. He tugged at a door but it held fast.

'Be The Woman of His Dreams!' He could hear his own feet pounding more slowly as he ran along the corridor. He grabbed at a doorknob as if he were about to fall into space. 'Enjoy Smoking Again, Thanks to This Secret Developed in Atomic Laboratories!' The knob fell off in his hand and he was running again.

'No Money Down!' a door shouted at him. He found it nailed tightly shut. The door next to it had no sign. Feeling his lungs about to

214

burst, Ryder took the doorknob in his hands and pulled with all the strength in him. The door flew open.

He was looking at himself sitting in a small, dingy room under an unshaded electric light bulb. He was dismantling a Colt .45 automatic pistol. He was oiling the parts and neatly placing each of them on a newspaper. A cockroach crawled across the paper and stopped for a moment on the headline.

'NOTHING...' the headline said, that part of it not covered up by pieces of the gun.

The cockroach tentatively touched the trigger mechanism, drew-back, froze for an instant, then scurried off the newspaper down the bed, across the floor and under the baseboard. The stench of gun oil filled the room and Ryder's nostrils. The cockroaches, he knew, would inherit the earth. Watching himself, he gestured to the him on the bed to uncover the headline. It seemed terribly important that he do so.

'NOTHING...' read the headline.

Ryder gestured impatiently and the other Ryder on the bed looked up. The reek of gun oil had become unbearable. Seeing him in the doorway, the Ryder on the bed raised his eyebrows and the Ryder at the door gestured to the newspaper again.

'*NOTHING* . . .'

Understanding him finally, the Ryder on the bed gently pushed aside the pieces of automatic pistol. The Ryder in the doorway could read the headline.

'*NOTHING TO BUY! 18 MONTHS TO PAY!*'

He awoke drenched in perspiration and shivering in the coolness from the Waldorf's air conditioning system. Sitting up in bed, he glanced at his watch. Twelve-fifty. An hour and ten minutes to K. The slash on his arm ached badly.

He sat there, shivering and wondering how soon the cockroaches would inherit the earth.

CHAPTER TWENTY-TWO

After a while he roused himself and went to a window. The brilliant blue sky shone so brightly over the boxy silhouettes of tall buildings, and glittered so dazzlingly in the sheets of glass that made up their walls, that for a moment Ryder had the illusion nothing could ever go wrong.

On such a day, he told himself, it just

wasn't possible that a man like Walt Connell—no matter how clever—could actually succeed.

He did not doubt that, given free access to these rooms, Connell could kill or badly maim K. But the incredible thought on a day like this was that Connell could then hope to become a kind of national hero, part sinner, part saint, the way Americans like their heroes.

'Nobody understands Americans the way I do,' Connell had told him once.

They had just said good night to a group of cell captains who had gathered at Connell's penthouse apartment for a social evening. Eight men, not counting Connell and Ryder, had emptied five fifths of whisky and finished a sirloin steak dinner. Connell had then called a very refined brothel a few blocks away where the madame sat waiting, girls assembled and ready.

As he watched the cell captains stumble over each other in their eagerness to leave Connell's apartment, Ryder decided there was probably enough material among the eight of them for one second-rate brain.

'God, Walt,' he complained. 'They're stupid.'

Connell sat with the phone still in his hand, so quickly had his underlings vacated the place. He showed the phone to Ryder. 'Want me to call that big blonde and her girlfriend?'

Ryder shook his head impatiently. 'How do you expect to pull off a thing as big as D-Day with an organization of lamebrains?'

'We're doing it, Johnny.'

'You can't count on idiots like them,' Ryder said. 'Five minutes after you drop that grenade, you'll be arrested. Those numbskulls will run for cover. You'll never hear from them again.'

'You just don't understand slobs, do you?' Connell asked patiently.

'I understand they're too stupid to be useful.'

'Nobody understands Americans the way I do, Johnny.' Connell replaced the phone in its cradle. 'Especially the way I understand American slobs.' He up-ended a whisky bottle over a glass and smiled when nothing came out. 'Anybody,' he mused, 'can build an organization of bright laddies. Bright laddies love to join things and work their way up. But anybody who builds with bright boys is doomed.'

He up-ended another bottle and found it

218

equally empty. 'But take my dummies. Out of the hundred I have in a hundred cities, there isn't one of my cell captains doesn't know I'm miles smarter than him. Just suppose I had a handful of brainy types, too. Out of a handful there'd be at least three with such pride in their own brains that they'd just naturally betray me to prove how smart they are.'

'I don't know, Walt, it doesn't sound . . .'

'I know,' Connell assured him. 'Dummies let me think for them. They know I'm better at it.'

'Just on the law of averages,' Ryder pointed out, 'you're bound to pick up a brainy type or two, even with that "mighty" and "insidious" line of yours.'

Connell laughed softly. 'Not one or two, Johnny. Just one. And why do you think you haven't been out of my sight in months, huh? You think I'm queer for boys or something? Sure, I gotta have one bright boy, but your kind of bright boy, Johnny, a special kind.'

Ryder's eyes narrowed slightly. 'What kind would that be?'

'I studied you,' Connell said. 'You're smart. But, like a lot of ex-newspaper men

219

you haven't got any real ambition. You're a natural follower. Give you a job and you do it great. But when I don't tell you what's next, you flounder. That's why I can afford the luxury of one bright boy, Johnny, your kind of bright boy.'

Neither of them spoke for a long moment, during which Ryder felt vaguely pleased that Connell had so accurately read the cover personality created for this assignment. Connell stared at him for a moment. 'Didn't know I had your number, huh?'

'Anybody who hooks up with you, Walt,' Ryder said, 'gets a strong dose of ambition. You've got it to spare.'

Connell's hoot of pleasure hurt Ryder's ears. 'You tell 'em, boy!' he crowed. 'I got ambition oozing out of my ears, the biggest ambition you ever saw and the simplest, too. All I want is this whole goddamned country on a silver platter.'

'Who's going to serve it up to you?'

Connell grinned. 'I spent years figuring this, Johnny. Traveled, talked to people, used my eyes and ears. I know this country as well as I know myself. This is a fat country, boy. The people are fat. We been living high off the sow-meat. We really

220

been living it up.'

'And you figure we're ready for a dose of austerity?'

'Hell, no.' Connell got up and moved restlessly about the living room, examining bottles for one with liquor left in it. 'We don't ever want the music to stop, Johnny. We want that hamfat gravy sluicing down on the mashed potatoes. We want the wheels to keep turning and the lights to keep burning and the money, money, money rolling in. That,' he stopped suddenly and shoved a thick finger at Ryder, 'that, young fella, is why we're all so scared.'

In the silence that followed. Connell found a partly-filled bottle and poured some whiskey in a glass. He swished the amber fluid around until it climbed up the inside of the glass and threatened to spill over the rim. 'Scared stiff,' he said then, more to himself than to Ryder. 'And there's nothing more disgusting than a fat man shaking with fright.'

He banged himself hard on the belly and swallowed half the whisky in the glass. 'I ain't exactly a skinny one, huh? I watch myself all the time. You've seen me. In mirrors. In the newsreels. I listen to myself on tape. And it ain't because I'm in love with the way I look or sound. Just this: the better I know me, the better I know this fat, sloppy country with all the fat, scared slobs in it.'

'You trying to tell me you're scared, Walt?'

'Not the way they are,' Connell admitted. 'They're sweaty-scared. I'm just careful-scared. Any smart man gets that way. How d'y'think I feel facing one of those howling mobs we collect in an auditorium? Do one thing wrong, one word, one gesture. Harp on something a minute too long. Any little thing can set them off, Johnny. Don't think I don't know it. And over the footlights they'd swarm, screaming for somebody's blood. We can't have that till we're good and ready. But every time I face 'em and feel that hate stirring in 'em, I'm scared, all right, plenty.'

Ryder held up his empty glass and watched Connell pour him a drink. 'What's your idea, Walt?' he asked. 'Stir them up just enough, till you're ready to turn them loose?'

Connell shook his head from side to side with an almost elephantine motion. He sat down on the long sofa across from Ryder and his head continued to shake. 'For all you're smart, Johnny,' he said at last, 'you're dumb where slobs are concerned. You never will understand 'em and that suits me fine.'

'But, I thought . . .'

'Thought?' Connell hooted. 'Never mind thinking, boy. You'll never understand them through your brain. I'll explain it to you, and you'll understand the words, but you'll never feel it down in your guts. The only way you'll ever know it is up here.' He tapped his head.

'You're what they call cerebral, Johnny,' he said. 'Even the way you handle yourself. I've seen you. You're handy with your mitts. But you learned it. With your head.' He patted his belly. 'Here's where I learn things, here in the gut. I feel it when it's right and when it's wrong. Now, you listen while I give you the words. Just understand the words, kid, 'cause you'll never feel them in your gut.'

Ryder sipped his whisky and wondered how much more of this bargain-basement psychoanalysis he would have to listen to. 'I'm listening, Walt,' he said then.

Connell nodded sagely. 'Then let's just

talk about one man, one fat, scared man. A man who's scared and skinny, now, is a man with nothing to lose. But a fat man's another story. He's got everything to lose. He's got his color TV, his big shiny car, his deep freeze, his electric dishwasher, his electric toothbrush, his electric can-opener, his son in college, his daughter's braces, his wife's mink—and a mortgage on the whole kit and kaboodle.

'Man, what he's got to lose. That's a big investment there. And when this man gets scared, Johnny, he freezes. I mean he actually sticks on the spot and don't know which way to turn. Nothing can budge him.

'Now multiply him by a few dozen million and you get a hefty chunk of this country,' Connell suggested. He smiled grimly and finished off his drink. 'Sure, we got skinny ones. We even got a few smart ones with enough backbone to brush their own teeth and open cans by hand. But mostly we got a nation of fat, lazy, scared slobs. And even the stupidest slob knows that the way things are right now is not the way they're gonna be. Even the dumbest knows everything's changing.

'They won't say it in so many words,

Johnny, because the words scare 'em even worse. But they all know what's happening. The blacks are rising in Africa; the yellows are rising in China; the reds are rising high in the sky right over our heads, halfway to the moon. And what's rising here? Nothing but the national debt.' He cackled suddenly, pleased with the thought. 'Remember that line, huh, kid? I'll use it in my next speech.'

'All right,' Ryder admitted. 'People are scared. And frightened people hate. But why does that make them follow you?'

'Me or somebody like me.'

'There's nobody like you,' Ryder said.

'Don't kid yourself,' Connell cautioned him. 'I ain't the only one to figure this out. The only thing I can claim is that I got a few new wrinkles to try out. Like D-Day, for instance.'

'That's another thing,' Ryder began. 'How can you expect them to . . .?'

'Listen to me,' Connell interrupted. 'Try to understand the words, boy. There was a time in this country when you wouldn't get anywhere stirring up the few fat slobs we used to have. But, today, right now, we got so many that they're the key to the whole thing.

'This country's like a big rock balanced on top of a mountain,' Connell explained. 'Unbalance it a little—by just the weight of a few fleas, maybe—and the rock'll roll whatever way you want it to. These scared slobs are my fleas, Johnny. I'm gonna march 'em over to one corner of the rock and bam-bamity-boom, down the mountain it'll roll. You watch.'

Ryder frowned. 'Forget these rocks and fleas. Walt. Let's talk practical talk. You're going to end up behind bars, a confessed assassin. Then you're going to sound a big rallying cry. What if nobody rallies to you?'

Connell's eyes had grown small as Ryder spoke. He seemed to be squinting into an intense fire whose flames danced to some future pattern. 'They will,' he murmured at last. 'The dumb slobs won't be able to help themselves.'

'With you behind bars?'

'What the hell difference does that make?' Connell asked irritably. 'The smartest thing the government could do is let me go. Let me walk the streets. Let everybody see I'm just another fat, sweaty slob. Feet of clay. But, behind bars, I'm a goddamned untouchable, martyr, Johnny. I'm everything people want me to be, everything I tell them I am. I'm anything at all, boy, because they can't see me.'

'I know how that works,' Ryder agreed. 'But it doesn't necessarily make them rally to you. Maybe just sympathize.'

'I'll settle for sympathy, to begin with,' Connell said. 'I intend to buy me a flock of legal appeals right up to the US Supreme Court. The whole thing could drag on for a couple of years, watch and see. And in those few years I'll turn sympathy into something stronger. Hell, boy, I got a defense that'll rock the nation.

'A simple idea for simple minds,' Connell went on. 'Just a simple question: Is a cold war really a war? Get the point? If it isn't a war, why the hell do we spend billions preparing for it? But if it is a war, then what I did with my little hand grenade was only what any other soldier does in wartime. Get it?'

'Neat,' Ryder lied. 'It'll shake a lot of people. But the prosecution won't let it faze them.'

'Hell difference's'it make what the prosecution says?' Connell asked. 'The trials don't mean a thing. It's the years of delay that count. I'll have me a coast-to-coast Save-Connell movement. I'll have people who never even heard of the Sons shelling out dimes and dollars for another underdog. Me. You know the way Americans are about underdogs.'

'Damn it, Walt,' Ryder complained. 'You're still talking about sympathy, not action. Just tell me one thing: why should they follow you?'

Connell's thick chuckle sounded like a powerful engine starting in chill weather. 'Because I mean something. Because I did something.'

'Doesn't make sense, Walt.'

'Ever save a drowning man?' Connell barked. 'First thing you do, you slug him. Any lifesaving course tells you that. Slug the bastard to show him you know what you're doing and he doesn't. A panicky man will understand only that, nothing else. He's stuck, frozen, paralyzed. The shock tells him, by God, if he wants to stay alive, he better do what you say.'

Ryder made a maybe-so face. 'What're you saying? The country's full of hysterics who need a slap in the face to set them straight?'

'Nuts! I'm saying the country's full of sick people ... so sick only strong medicine'll cure 'em. And they know it.'

'Cure them,' Ryder mused, 'and kill you.'

Connell laughed. 'Don't worry so much about the Old Man, Johnny. There's a risk, but I've got it figured.'

'Some gamble, Walt. Your life is the stake.'

'Just listen, kid, listen and learn. We've got our Save-Connell movement rolling, see.' Connell began to move about restlessly, starting now to act out his dream. 'Pretty soon it isn't just to save one fat martyr. Pretty soon it has an organizational backbone. Within a few weeks after D-Day it's already taking shape and building every day into what'll end up the biggest political force in the country.'

'Bigger than the two regular parties?'

'Who said anything about a political party?' Connell asked.

'I thought . . .'

'A political party is a handful of bright boys who work all year and a big gob of slobs who flock to the polls at election time. A political force is something else, Johnny. It works 365 days a year, slobs and all. Every day of the year they have orders to carry out.' He poked a finger at Ryder. 'Orders from you.'

'What kind of orders could I...?'

'The ones I give you,' Connell cut in. 'The ones I give my cadre.'

Ryder thought for a moment. 'I can see how it might work,' he said then. 'The Sons serve as your backbone for the Save-Connell movement and pretty soon it's all one big force. But what happens when you lose the last appeal?'

'Pay day!'

'I don't...'

'The big payoff, Johnny,' Connell crowed. 'Raising money and holding rallies is all fine and dandy. But there comes a time when these phony tigers of mine gotta have raw meat to sink their teeth in.'

'And that happens when the last appeal is turned down?'

'I envy you, boy,' Connell said, 'being on the outside to see the whole thing happen.' He was pacing the room now, gesturing like a hypnotist as he began to conjure up his visions.

'I don't know the name of the town where it'll happen, Johnny. It could be any town, wherever they've got me locked up waiting for the last appeal. The Supreme Court's about to announce their decision. Thousands of people have been flocking into Town X; they're converging from all over the country in caravans, motorcades. The town's busting at the seams. Violence builds, a little at a time. First off, the picket line around the jail gets too big for the cops to handle. Then you get little isolated events: Pickets shove cops, cops shove pickets; A car gets overturned; Some windows get smashed; A street fight here; Slogans plastered on walls all over town. Now you tramp your toe down on the accelerator and give it all you got: Power failure; Gas main explosion; Four-alarm fire in an empty loft building. Whatever way you can tie up Town X, you do it, even to traffic jams. You're in high gear now and there's nothing stopping you. The town's tied in a knot. You blow a bridge. Raid a TV station. Bing! Bang! The cops and the FBI and the firemen all running round in circles trying to cope. Then the one-two haymaker. One! A dynamiting of a bank or an airport control tower or something. You wait just long enough for the alarm to drain cops out of the center of town or wherever the jail is. Then . . . two! You blow the jail. I crash out with another prisoner, anybody who's got my build. A helicopter hovers over the jail, darts down, snatches the other guy and zooms away. I slip into a car and make my way slowly out of town. The cops chase the helicopter. By the time they down it, I'm two states away in hiding. And that's where I stay. Nobody sees me. Nobody touches me. Just my cadre. I'm here. I'm there. I'm everywhere. In weeks I'm a legend. You know how it works, Johnny. In weeks, I'm . . . a legend.'

The big man paused and drew a deep, unsteady breath. Ryder watched the tension slowly subside in Connell's heavy body. 'That's quite a dream, Walt,' he said at last.

'I dream big,' Connell said, his voice husky. 'But you and I know it's more than a pipedream. Feed that kind of raw meat to my tigers, Johnny, and there's no holding 'em Because nothing . . . nothing succeeds like success.'

Over the clear blue sky of Park Avenue, as Ryder stood now at the Waldorf window staring with blind eyes at the scene below, a sudden movement across the sky caught his attention and wrenched his mind out of the past and into the present.

A green-white-and-black police heli-copter hovered over the Avenue well above the building tops. Ryder caught a flash of sunlight reflected from binoculars someone in the cockpit was holding. He turned from the window, feeling faintly sick to his stomach.

So vividly had he recreated Connell in his mind's eye that the emotional power of the man had almost laid hold of him now as it had that night in Chicago. Ryder found himself wondering again whether Connell were right, whether he could really become the hero he planned to be.

Grimacing, Ryder headed for the bathroom, stripping off clothing. He stepped into the shower and turned it on full force.

CHAPTER TWENTY-THREE

After he had showered, he felt a great deal better. He swallowed a dexedrine tablet, changed to his clean underwear and shirt, then put on the trousers of the olive green suit.

Whether it was the nearness of the conclusion or the dexedrine, he felt no need for food, although he had eaten only a sandwich in the last twenty-four hours. In itself, he realized, this was unusual. The work he did rarely affected his appetite for food or liquor. He had learned to keep his professional tensions walled off from the rest of him, at least until recently.

Standing at the Park Avenue windows, he noted that the police had carefully insulated the street from the sidewalk with a double row of wooden horses, except for a six-foot gap directly in front of the main entrance. Watching two mounted police stepping their horses very slowly back and forth along the barricade, Ryder was struck with the sudden thought that, until Connie had come back into his life, he had been able successfully to wall off his tensions from the rest of him because there had been nothing much to the rest of him, just a body and a few half-forgotten reflexes.

He shook his head, angry at himself for introspecting this close to showdown. It had to stop. He pushed his mind onto something else, anything at all . . . Peter.

Probably drugged and tied up somewhere, Ryder decided. Not dead yet because it would be too hard for Sovint to pass off. But as good as dead, certainly.

Another good man on an errand of uselessness. And yet, he thought, his nothing makes my nothing important, just as mine makes his necessary. Without each other, neither of us would exist. It was one of science's most recent discoveries, anti-matter. Peter and I, he told himself, are anti-matter. Take one away and the other vanishes. And what a lot of money it would save the taxpayers.

The poor, miserable, lied-to, hyped-up taxpayers.

He turned abruptly from the window, furious at the knowledge that he could not stop himself from this dangerous interior inspection. He knew that what he should now be doing was working out a way of keeping Connell out of Ponamarenko's hands until after the summit conference had ended. Instead he was trapped with one thought, circling in his head like a dog biting his own tail.

Two highly-trained, well-educated men, he kept thinking, involved in paper chases and hide-and-seek games that have meaning only in the act of cancelling each other out. The waste of all the men and women and time and lives and money, the terrible waste merely to achieve cancellation.

Someone knocked on the door.

Ryder slipped on his shoes and checked quickly about him for a proper weapon. If this were Connell, off schedule for some reason, now was as good a time to put him out of the way as later. 'Just a second,' he called to the closed door. He hefted a cut-glass, narrow-necked flower vase and found it both heavy and handy enough.

Placing it on an end table, he went to the door and opened it. Ponamarenko's huge bulk filled the doorway. 'Excuse,' he said, pursing his small, plump-lipped mouth, 'again I must bother you.'

'No bother at all,' Ryder said cheerfully, not yielding an inch at the doorway. 'What can I do for you?'

'I should like to have talk with you,' Ponamarenko said in very cautious English. 'Private.'

'What's the beef, friend,' Ryder asked, smiling.

'Private, please?' Ponamarenko responded, moving into the room.

'Now, buddy,' Ryder said, still smiling. 'I'm expecting a visitor if you know what I mean.' He winked.

'I know this,' the big man assured him. He felt himself somewhere around his great, but not flabby, midriff. When his hand appeared again it dwarfed a .38 revolver. 'I expect also this visitor,' he said.

Ryder moved back from the door. The big man surged in.

The door closed behind him without his having touched it and Ryder realized that someone was behind Bullneck. 'You got a boy on your back, pal,' Ryder pointed out.

Grinning pleasantly, Peter stepped out from behind Ponamarenko and showed Ryder a snub-nosed .32. 'You look very rested,' he said in a friendly manner. 'I am glad you slept.' The skin under one eye, recently purple, looked pink and healthy again.

'What are y—?' Ryder felt his throat choke back the question as the answer suddenly became apparent.

'What is it you say here?' Peter asked amiably. 'If you can't lick them, join them? Yes. So I am here.'

Ryder turned slowly and went to the couch. He sat down, not looking at the two men, not wanting them to see the look of betrayal he felt sure was on his face. And I was worried about Peter, he thought. Hell!

'Ah-h-h,' Peter said in a commiserating tone, 'you feel badly. But, my friend, it is the only realistic way. At least now we will be certain that this job gets done.' He smiled again. 'Connell's job . . . not yours.'

CHAPTER TWENTY-FOUR

At a little after one-thirty, Peter turned on the television set and found a channel that was broadcasting the arrival procession. As he tuned it in, Ryder could see a long shot of the United Nations Plaza, flags flapping lazily in a gentle August breeze off the river.

The shot switched to a telephoto one and he could see K alighting from his open car, and marching up a short, shallow flight of steps holding a wreath in his hands. He was flanked by two men on his left, huskies whose purpose was obvious, and a thin man in horn-rimmed spectacles on his right. No microphones had been placed at the location of the wreath presentation, but after K had put down the wreath, he turned and made his way to a cluster of microphones almost at the curb of First Avenue.

'Sir,' a television reporter was shouting, 'can you tell us what you expect to result

238

from this summit conference?'

K reached the microphones and beamed at the crowd of people separated from him by a good fifty feet of sidewalk. He fired off a burst of Russian and the thin, bespectacled man cleared his throat.

'It is with a great deal of pleasure that I come again to your miraculous city,' he said. After another series of sentences in Russian, he continued: 'You are to be congratulated on this remarkable architectural achievement which . . .'

The rest of the interpreter's words were drowned out by reporters begging for information on the conference. K's smallish eyes twinkled in the hot August sunlight. He spoke again. 'A momentous event in international history is about to unfold,' the interpreter said. 'It is the crowning achievement of my life that I am alive to play a part in it.'

'Counting his chickens,' Peter said quietly, 'before they are hatched.'

'. . . In amity and peace between the peoples of our two great nations,' the interpreter concluded. The reporters began firing questions again, but this time, smile off, K and his entourage strode briskly back to the motorcade.

Peter checked his watch. 'On time,' he announced. 'A magnificent example of how punctuality can lead to one's downfall.'

Ponamarenko's tiny mouth relaxed and assayed a small smile. He asked Peter something in Russian, which Ryder translated as a suggestion that Ryder be rendered unconscious at once.

'No need for the mother tongue,' Peter assured the big man. 'Sergeant Ryder, I am sure, took conversational Russian at the New York City Police Department's famous training academy.'

'. . . We take you now to our cameras at the intersection of Forty-seventh Street and Park Avenue,' the announcer was saying. The motorcade moved out of sight along First Avenue, heading uptown. The street was deserted and, for a moment, Ryder caught sight of a line of mounted police holding back traffic.

'Tell your fat friend why I have to remain conscious,' Ryder asked.

'I'm surprised,' Peter said. 'That isn't fat. Show him, Comrade Ponamarenko.'

The big man shrugged and threw his arms out wide. One of his fists caught Ryder in the side of the face and knocked him sprawling across the couch.

The two Russians chuckled appreciatively, 'Although he cannot judge muscle,' Peter commented, 'he is a fairly good tactician, in a rudimentary fashion. He's right, Ponamarenko. He must admit Connell, he and no one else.'

'But will he?' the big man wanted to know.

'He cannot afford to let Connell run unchecked about the hotel, hatching new plots. Even though he knows why we are here, he will have to cooperate and usher Connell in.'

'What do you do with me after you make sure Connell drops the grenades?' Ryder asked. 'Ever thought about that? The Police Department will blow this wide open if you claim I was a real assassin.'

Ponamarenko chuckled again, a small, muffled sound like a clogged toilet bowl. 'You will be found much later,' he said. 'You will be . . . what is the word, Pyotr?'

'Unidentifiable,' Peter finished for him. 'A beautiful word? Beautiful. It has a tempo to it, like the beat of marching feet. Un-iden-tifi-able.'

'. . . Moving slowly west on Forty-seventh Street now,' the television announcer was saying. Ryder watched some blurs that could have been anything grow very slightly larger on the screen. He glanced at his watch. One-forty-five.

Unidentifiable, he thought. Everything becomes that in the end. He nursed the side of his face where the big man had belted him. It was so easy, he thought, to identify Peter as a good professional with the right instincts, because you saw yourself in him. That was your big mistake. He isn't like you and he never will be in a million years. He's a new breed of cat. You were a damned stupid fool for ever unwrapping yourself to him and you'll pay for that stupidity with your life.

Nevertheless, Ryder told himself, it made killing Peter almost enjoyable.

That there would be bloodshed now was clear. The fact that only killing Peter and the big man would leave him free to immobilize Connell made their deaths necessary. The fact that Ryder might die in the attempt to kill two armed men was also plain to see. But the fact that they would conclude today's adventure by killing him made his attempt necessary. Oh, he decided, the logic is pretty steely, all right.

'. . . Turning the corner onto Park Avenue,' the announcer said.

They had a telephoto lens trained on K's car and Ryder could see him wave to the hundreds of people who lined the route. Between him and the people was a layer of Sovint guards, a row of mounted New York police and a line of patrolmen maintaining the double wooden barricade. Yet K's gestures were calm. He looked quite at ease in his posture of triumph.

What the hell, Ryder asked himself, what is so tremendous about him that I must die to keep him alive? If his own people want him dead, who am I to give my life in defying them?

'Pick up the phone and report two bulbs blown out,' Peter ordered.

Silently, Ryder moved to the phone. His best bet was to make the call and, as he hung up, to duck into the bedroom and barricade the door. Peter's analysis of his thinking, as expressed to Bullneck, was way off the mark. Rather than let Connell into the suite, Ryder would risk having him run loose in the hotel. For once, Peter had been outguessed.

'Operator?' he said. 'There's two light bulbs blown out here and I can't read. Will you send up an electrician?' He waited for her answer, then hung up. As he replaced

243

the phone he swung casually through half a turn toward the bedroom door.

'Continue to turn one more fraction of an inch,' Peter remarked, 'and I will put a bullet through your shoulder.' He raised the gun and took careful aim.

'With that toy?' Ryder asked. 'It's too inaccurate.'

'I will be better,' Ponamarenko guaranteed. 'Believe this.' His little mouth was pursed so tight that the lips looked white.

'. . . Crossing Forty-eighth Street now and the motorcade is beginning to slow down. In a few moments, it will reach the Waldorf, ladies and gentlemen.' Ryder moved back into the center of the living room.

'All right!' he snapped. 'Let the son of a bitch die!'

Ponamarenko blinked. He lowered his gun. 'You cooperate?'

'Why the hell shouldn't I?' Ryder asked. He could feel his heart pounding hard against his ribs. He tensed himself for the final move. 'What's he to me? If you want him dead, I say, let him die.'

Ryder fell forward, pushing with all the strength in his legs, until his shoulder chopped into the big man's legs right at the knees. He felt the immense frame start to buckle and he scrambled sideways on the floor, using Ponamarenko as a shield from Peter while he grabbed for the big man's gun.

As his fingers closed over the gun, he felt it whip out of his grasp. Ponamarenko jumped to his feet. 'Enough,' he said angrily. 'This one dies now.'

Lying at his feet, Ryder saw one meaty finger whiten at the knuckle as Ponamarenko started to squeeze the trigger.

There was a sharp, furious pop, like the sound of a small dog barking. Ponamarenko's fingers buried themselves in his stomach. He began to fold up in a huge bundle on the floor. Ryder glanced at Peter, who was pocketing his snub-nosed .32.

'Quickly,' Peter said. 'Help me lug this pig out of sight.'

Panting with the exertion, they moved the big man's body just inside the bedroom. From the living room came two quick knocks on the door.

Peter nodded and closed the bedroom door, hiding both himself and the body. As the door closed, his eyes caught Ryder's again in that same direct, level stare.

Ryder took a long, steadying breath and wiped his hands on the sides of his trousers. '. . . Cars are stopping now,' the announcer was saying.

Ryder walked to the front door and let Connell in.

CHAPTER TWENTY-FIVE

They sat in the dim, dingy back room at P. J. Clarke's bar on Third Avenue in the tiny alcove at the far rear, the two of them drinking Michelob, newspapers spread about on the heavy round table between them. Bright young people in twos and fours were beginning to fill the place for an after-five martini and both Ryder and Peter realized that it would soon be unsafe to talk here. In a few minutes they would each get up and go their separate ways.

'Did the hotel seem disturbed about Connell?' Peter asked quietly.

'Not a murmur. I doused him with cheap rye and left him smelling up the corridor near the elevators. He's probably sleeping off the last of the Seconal in that basement lockup you're so fond of.'

'A man blind drunk in the Waldorf,' Peter said and shook his head. 'Such a thing staggers the imagination.'

Ryder swallowed some of the cool Michelob and closed his eyes for a moment. His opportunities to sleep in the last three days had been sporadic. He glanced across at Peter, who was reading reports on the conference's closing session in the *Times*. He hadn't actually seen the man since three days before, when Peter had contrived to remove Ponamarenko's dead bulk with the efficiency of someone who had worked for sixteen months in the Waldorf and had discovered at least three ways of meeting such a situation. The contusion area under Peter's eye looked grey-brownish now and much smaller in size. Spotty remnants of makeup failed to lessen its prominence and Ryder realized that Peter must have been moving so fast in the last three days that he had neglected to freshen the pancake makeup over the discolored skin.

'You got through to your folks over there?'

Peter nodded, absorbed in the *Times*. Still reading, he reached for his beer. 'All taken care of,' he muttered. 'They know all about it.'

'And the proper people have been liquidated?'

Peter frowned and looked up from the *Times*. 'My dear sir,' he said then, 'you are living in another era. We cannot do it the good old way any more. Times have changed. You would do well to keep up with them.'

Nodding, Ryder sipped his beer. 'Pardon me,' he said. 'When are they scheduled for unimportant posts in out-of-the-way and extremely frigid locales?'

'That,' Peter put down the *Times*, 'is not for me to decide.' Raising his glass, he inclined his head toward Ryder. '*Nazdarovya.*'

'*Spasibo.*'

As he drank, Ryder looked casually about him and noted that the nearest couple was still three tables away. 'I trust,' he said in a low voice, 'that on your return home, K will reward you properly for your intrepid devotion to duty.'

'He doesn't know I exist,' Peter said. 'And as far as I am concerned, we can all keep it that way.' One corner of his mouth quirked up oddly. 'What kind of bonus will

248

you receive?'

'A vacation, I hope.'

'With pay?'

'Peter, this is still America. Of course with pay.'

'Yoi!' Peter picked up the *Times* and resumed his reading. The two men sat in silence for a long moment. A couple sat down two tables away. Peter sighed and folded his newspaper. Their privacy was ending.

'Well,' he said and sighed again. 'We will probably meet again in the next few years across the barrels of loaded guns.' He pushed away from the table and stared down at the floor. 'I hope not.'

'I can guarantee we won't,' Ryder told him. 'I'm resigning.'

Peter's thick eyebrows went up. 'So? It is permitted?'

'They'll argue, but they can't stop me.'

'What are your plans then?'

Ryder shrugged. 'I must have an awful lot of money banked in my name. I'll give myself a year to unkink and another year or two to find out who I am and what I want to do. No hurry.'

'You are serious.'

'Very.'

'Why?' Peter asked. 'I should like very much to know.'

'You already know,' Ryder assured him. 'I've started introspecting too much, asking myself too many questions, the usual signs of decay you begin to see in yourself. If I stuck at it I'd become a liability. They'd have to ease me into a desk slot where I could bend and unbend paper clips for the rest of my life.'

'It makes too much sense.'

'So I'll retire with my reputation and ego in one piece.' Ryder moistened his lips, not liking the sound of what he was about to suggest, but wanting to say it anyway. The brief moment of indecision was unique for him. He began to realize all the responsibilities of choice he would face when he elected to live his own life freely again. He took a breath and spoke.

'Why don't you bow out, too?' he asked Peter.

Peter's lower lip came out. 'It's a subject,' he said after a moment, 'that has occupied too many of my thoughts recently.'

'You know,' Ryder said, 'in the war, when you had flown your fifty missions, you could be sent back home. Both of us have flown our fifty missions ... and more.' Ryder paused and lowered his voice to a more prudent level. 'We've earned the right to return to normal living again.'

'But,' Peter asked slowly, 'do we want to?'

'I do.'

'To live like a normal person? Play no roles? To hide behind no false façades? To make one's own decisions? It is a frightening prospect.'

Ryder felt his heart slow in sudden fear, then bound ahead too quickly. 'Frightening,' he agreed. 'But people do it. I keep telling myself that everyone else knows who he is and accepts responsibility for what he does. I keep telling myself this...' He broke off and lowered his voice again. 'I have to try it,' he said then. 'Just as I was about to, the war came along and ... and all this. I don't know what will happen, but I have to find out now, soon, before I'm too old for it.'

'I wish you great strength and good luck,' Peter said after a moment.

'Why not you, too?' Ryder asked. 'You've got your citizenship papers here. Just drop the whole thing and start out new in this country.'

'No good.'

'Why?'

Peter took a quick swallow of the Michelob. 'Just no good,' he repeated. 'I cannot live a private life here. It would be much easier at home than here, actually.'

'It's a big country.'

Peter nodded. 'So is mine.' He licked his upper lip to remove the thin line of foam. 'I have accumulated almost a year's leave,' he said then. 'I shall spend it at home, where no one really knows what I am . . . or was. Then, we'll see. But to strike roots here . . . no. I would never feel right. I have a country of my own, my friend. And if I can find another way to do something for it, I will. Who knows,' he said in a suddenly brighter tone, 'I may go into politics.'

Laughing, they both finished their beers. For a moment neither of them made a move to leave. Ryder toyed with the idea as he had for the past three days, of thanking Peter for saving his life, not just the final act of shooting Ponamarenko, but the strategy of pretending to join forces with the big man in order to keep him from killing Ryder. So thinking he looked across the table at Peter and decided that would be too awkward between professionals on

252

opposite sides.

They got to their feet.

Ryder looked down at the debris on the table top, newspapers black with headlines and grim-faced pictures. 'Summit Meeting Ends in Stalemate,' the *Times* put it; 'No Basis for Agreement Found.' The *News* did it more succinctly: REDS SINK SUMMIT PARLEY.' The *Post's* one-word front page asked: 'WHY?'

Walking past the long bar and out into the late sunlight along Third Avenue, the two men paused at the corner and looked at the sidewalk for an instant.

'So,' Peter said then, keeping his tone light, 'it's all over and it all ends in nothing.'

Ryder watched him for a moment and then held out his hand. 'Not quite,' he said in a tone that matched Peter's. 'Not quite.'

They shook hands and walked off in different directions without looking back.

CHAPTER TWENTY-SIX

Ryder stepped into a public phone booth at the corner of Fifty-first Street and Third

253

Avenue, examined the change in his pocket and found that he had enough.

He dialled the 703 code and a Virginia number, then paid the operator what he owed her. After the phone had rung several times, a man answered.

'Have Charlie call Mr. Rutherford at the Waldorf,' Ryder said.

'Pardon me?'

Ryder heard the recording device cut in on the line. 'Tell Charlie to call Mr. Rutherford at the Waldorf,' he repeated.

'Nice and quiet up your way, Pigeon,' the man said.

'Very.'

'Want to talk to Charlie's house guest, huh?'

'That's the general idea.'

'Can do. She's still there.'

'Man, you've got a big mouth.'

The man at the other end laughed briefly. 'Bye-bye, Pidge.'

Ryder hung up, left the booth and started toward Lexington Avenue at a rapid pace. He wanted to reach his room in time for the phone call.

Photoset, printed and bound in Great Britain by REDWOOD BURN LIMITED, Trowbridge, Wiltshire